## "How much do I owe you, Doc?" Greg asked softly.

Going along with the joke, Diane said, "Nothing, it's part of the Holiday Homes service."

"But I insist on paying," he said persuasively and folded her in his arms. "Oh, Diane, my dearest," he murmured. "How can I give you up?"

He tightened his embrace, ravaging her lips and her face and her neck with kisses. Feverishly, he undid the top button of her shirt and continued until her soft, breasts lay under his hands. His mouth astride hers in a long, pulsing kiss, his fingers caressed the straining breasts in motions that made her nerves sing with excitement...

Dear Reader:

Two months ago we were delighted to announce the arrival of TO HAVE AND TO HOLD, the thrilling new romance series that takes you into the world of married love. We're pleased to report that letters of praise and enthusiasm are pouring in daily. TO HAVE AND TO HOLD is clearly off to a great start!

TO HAVE AND TO HOLD is the first and only series that portrays the joys and heartaches of marriage. Its unique concept makes it significantly different from the other lines now available to you, and it presents stories that meet the high standards set by SECOND CHANCE AT LOVE. TO HAVE AND TO HOLD offers all the compelling romance, exciting sensuality, and heartwarming entertainment you expect.

We think you'll love TO HAVE AND TO HOLD—and that you'll become the kind of loyal reader who is making SECOND CHANCE AT LOVE an ever-increasing success. Read about love affairs that last a lifetime. Look for three TO HAVE AND TO HOLD romances each and every month, as well as six SECOND CHANCE AT LOVE romances each month. We hope you'll read and enjoy them all. And please keep writing! Your thoughts about our books are very important to us.

Warm Wishes,

*Ellen Edwards*

Ellen Edwards
SECOND CHANCE AT LOVE
The Berkley Publishing Group
200 Madison Avenue
New York, N.Y. 10016

# MIDSUMMER MAGIC
# KATE NEVINS

A
SECOND CHANCE AT LOVE
BOOK

# - 1 -

THE HARD-PACKED YELLOW sand was cold under her bare feet. The gray drizzle, the famous Breton *bruine*, wet her upturned face and curled the tendrils of tawny hair that escaped from her sweat-shirt hood.

It was still only June and she had the beach to herself. The French families wouldn't arrive for another week, when school let out. Then the blue and white striped tents would go up, facing the emerald water of the bay. The children would come to the Seagulls Club, shake hands with the teacher, and spend the morning in supervised beach games while their mothers blanketed the sand with the crimson and navy yarn of next winter's sweaters. And the university students would read Hemingway in English, turning the pages slowly.

But now there was nobody—no one in the villas that the company she worked for rented to vacationers in the little resort town of Saint-Cast; no one at her Aunt Yvonne's house except herself; no one even in her life except Lyle, thousands of miles away in Forestville, Illinois. And running alone under the gray Breton sky, her legs swift and sure

1

under her, Diane James had the eerie feeling that she could well be the only person left on earth.

She was now almost at the point in her morning run where the crescent beach ended at one of the two headlands that embraced the bay, like arms reaching out into the water. The Channel beyond was still shrouded in mist, but the rain had stopped and the bay itself was clear.

A flash of movement in the water caught her eye, but only for a moment. She was tiring and turned her attention back to the beach, measuring with a glance the distance remaining to her self-imposed goal. Halfway to that point was a pile of clothes she hadn't noticed before.

The cold green water off this northernmost coast of France didn't usually attract swimmers so early in the season. Her heart began to race with fear. Was there a suicide out there?

She stared out across the water again. A surge of relief swept over her. A dark head was cutting the waves in the purposeful motions of an experienced swimmer. Even so, she waited just in case. She looked again at the clothes— a pair of neatly folded chinos, sandals, a white T-shirt, Jockey shorts, and a striped beach towel.

When she returned her gaze to the water, a nude male figure was striding out of the surf, broad shouldered, with a powerful chest and narrow hips. White foam flecked the strong brown legs, and his hair was dark and curly, like a Mediterranean god's.

*"Allez-vous-en!"* the man shouted at her in an unmistakable American accent.

The embarrassment Diane felt evaporated in an irresistible urge to laugh. What would this fellow American do if she just stood there and pretended she hadn't understood his command to go away? Ducking her head to hide her amusement, Diane turned and ran across the sand to the short flight of stairs leading up to the concrete boardwalk.

Who was he? So far as she knew, she was the only American in Saint-Cast.

\* \* \*

Her first stop after her morning run was always the hole-in-the-wall bakery where, at that hour, she had to shout *"Mademoiselle!"* three times, like the magical calls in a fairy tale, before a sleepy-eyed teenager with long, dark, tangled hair came out to the bakery counter from the living quarters behind. But today it was the girl's father, the floury-armed baker himself, who handed Diane her *baguette,* a two-foot-long rod of golden bread, which she tucked under her arm, and two *pains au chocolat,* still warm and oozing bittersweet chocolate, in a waxed-paper bag.

Outside on the street, the smell of the warm bread and the chocolate-filled rolls was tantalizing. Diane took a roll from the bag and bit into it. Some of the fragrant chocolate oozed out, and she rummaged in her pocket for a tissue, casually wiped her mouth, then continued eating.

Pushing back her hood, she shook out her reddish-gold hair as she sauntered along to her second regular stop, the little bookstore where her copy of the *International Herald Tribune,* the only one to come to Saint-Cast, was always waiting to be carried back to her aunt's house and savored with a big cup of *café au lait* and her second chocolate-filled roll. Diane read the French papers, too, but her day didn't start until she had read the *"Trib."*

Amused, she thought of the American swimmer again. Like her, he must have thought he was all alone in that world of sea and sand. Poor fellow, what a shock her sudden appearance had been for him! She laughed softly. Whoever he was, he was a beautiful man. Wet, glistening skin. Powerful chest matted with dark, wiry hair. Thigh muscles taut from swimming.

Still smiling, still slightly chocolaty even after several wipes of the tissue, she reached the bookstore just as the Mediterranean god was leaving. Only now, chinos and T-shirt were stretched tight over the muscle and sinew she had seen in their pristine state.

The Mediterranean god had a newspaper folded under his arm. Diane glanced at it. The print was familiar. The words that sprang out at her were English.

With a cry of anguish, she sprinted toward him and placed herself directly in his path.

"That's *my* paper!"

Dark brows shot up in surprise. Then his deep-set brown eyes glinted with amusement. "I know you! You're the Peeping Tom from the beach."

Diane flushed. "Hardly! That's a public beach. *You* were the one at fault." She put her hand out. "I'd like my paper, please. Monsieur Aubert orders the *Trib* for me every day and keeps it until I pick it up."

With an expression of feigned innocence, he said, "So *that's* what that Frenchman was trying to tell me."

Diane gave him a disdainful look and stuck out her hand again. "My paper, please."

He ignored her hand. The dark eyes scanned hers.

"You have gray eyes."

"So?"

"With red hair?"

"It's not a genetic impossibility," she answered tartly. "Besides, my hair's more blond than red. And *now* may I have my paper?"

"You're not French."

"No," she said shortly.

The probing, amused eyes left her face then and traveled slowly over the emphatic curves beneath the navy jogging suit, returning to rest on the white cotton Portuguese fisherman's scarf she had wound around her neck.

"I've never seen a jogger wrapped up like a Dickensian caroler."

She shrugged. "I'm a singer, and the dampness is bad for my throat." She reached out and slid the newspaper from under his arm. "Thank you so much."

His dark eyes gleamed. A smile twitched at the corners of his firm mouth.

"You have chocolate on your face."

Still? she thought ruefully. She made a slight motion with her hand to wipe it off, but he was ahead of her.

"Here, use this." He reached into a pocket and handed her a large, very white handkerchief.

As she took it, the *baguette* started to slip. She grabbed the bread, and the newspaper fell on the wet sidewalk.

"Thank *you* very much." He picked up the paper, nonchalantly thrust it under his arm, and walked away.

Diane boiled over with anger. The nerve of him! The colossal, unmitigated nerve! She followed him with long, efficient strides. Smiling, but with a serrated edge to her voice, she said, "I still have your handkerchief. And that's more than ever my paper."

"More than ever?"

"More than ever," she repeated, wondering at the same time about her logic, "because the French police would be very interested to hear about a man skinny-dipping at a public beach. This isn't a nudist camp on the Riviera, you know."

"You're telling me," he muttered, with an upward look at the cloudy sky.

She held her hand out, palm upturned. "Well, how about my paper?"

A grin creased his tanned face.

"Suppose we share it?" He indicated the paper bag in her hand. "You've got the Danish, or should I say 'French,' and I'll supply the coffee."

She hesitated. Then curiosity made her ask, "Where are you staying?"

"I'm renting. I believe the house belongs to a family called Poilvet."

"But you *can't* be at the Poilvets'!" she objected. "No one told me."

The pleasant smile yielded to a quizzical look.

"I'm the area representative—or courier, as it's called here—for Holiday Homes International," Diane explained. "I'm staying in my aunt's house while she's away. She's French. My mother was French and my dad, American; so I'm bilingual," she said in further explanation, immediately wondering why she had given him this information about herself. "I know the Poilvets placed their house with us for a summer rental," she went on, "but I'm supposed to be informed when someone moves into a villa. It's my job to see that everything is all right and to offer my help, particularly to people who don't speak French. And nobody told me you were moving into the Poilvet house."

She eyed him suspiciously. Was he some kind of squatter who had broken into the house? It was strange, his going for a swim in that cold water and having only a T-shirt and pants to wear on a chilly morning.

"Holiday Homes is the firm I dealt with." His eyes were laughing at her again, and the easy, relaxed look had returned to his face.

"Then why didn't either our London or New York office let me know?" she asked sharply.

"There probably wasn't time. I called your London office from Paris yesterday, asked if a house was available in Saint-Cast, and put the whole thing on a credit card. Then I rented a car, drove here, and arrived early in the evening."

Her glance pointedly swept his clothes again.

"I've just come back from Africa," he said softly. "Being cool for a change—even cold—feels good."

That story might account for his deep tan and early-morning swim, Diane thought, but was no assurance he had a right to be in the Poilvet house. Her look remained stern.

His lips twitched slightly with amusement. "The man I talked to in London was named Pentwhistle," he said. "Hilary Pentwhistle. You know I couldn't have made up a name like that."

Diane laughed. "You win. Too bad you didn't meet Hilary. The appearance goes with the name."

"Thin strands of dark hair combed carefully over a bald head? Or a toupee like badly laid carpet?"

She laughed again, a rich, musical sound. "The toupee, *plus* a pince-nez on a long black string." Then she frowned slightly. "Is the house in order? If I had known, I would have checked it out. That's part of my job."

"Looks good to me," he said heartily.

"How about help? Would you like me to arrange for someone to come in to clean and cook for you?"

He shook his head. "I'm an experienced bachelor."

"In cooking and cleaning?" she asked dubiously.

"In everything," he answered smoothly.

But she hardly heard his answer. She was intrigued by this big, easygoing demigod who had come to Saint-Cast from Africa. Why Saint-Cast? And what had he been doing in Africa? Then her sense of responsibility reasserted itself and she ran through her mind the things she should be telling this unexpected client of Holiday Homes.

"You know, the wind off the Channel can be very strong. No one here ever opens the windows and doors of a room at the same time, since this creates a draft that can shatter the windows. I had to go over to Val-André only yesterday because an English family had done that very thing and thought they shouldn't have to pay for the window that broke. They called it a 'natural occurrence,' but I had warned them, so they had to replace the window pane."

"Scout's honor, I won't break any of the Poilvets' windows," he said solemnly.

"Also, if you get sick . . ."

"You'll come and take care of me?" he interrupted eagerly.

"I'll get you a doctor," she said sternly. "In other words, if an emergency arises or anything comes up in connection with the house, you're supposed to call me, the area representative of Holiday Homes."

"Shouldn't you be a little more cautious about making that offer?"

"What do you mean?"

"Well, I foresee all kinds of emergencies—the tub running over and ruining the Poilvets' rugs, the electric wiring coming apart and causing a fire, the flock of sheep I've seen a shepherd lead past the house breaking in. You might be getting a call a day from me."

She didn't answer. They had turned back toward the beach and were walking through the strip of pines behind it. The carpet of rust-red pine needles made the sandy path slippery, and Diane's old sandals were worn almost smooth, so she had to concentrate on not falling. But finally she decided she could risk a haughty look, and said icily, "I hardly think those eventualities will occur."

His bright, dark eyes brimmed with merriment. "You're not very friendly about it."

"Holiday Homes does not go in for friendship. It is a large, cold, impersonal organization, Mr. . . . I don't think I got your name."

"I didn't give it," he answered smoothly. "Why do you work for a large, cold, impersonal organization?" he said, mimicking her. All the while his eyes lingered on her red-blond hair and glowing skin. "You don't seem the type."

"For money, I suppose," she said mockingly. Then her eyes laughed back at him. "Pittance that it is." She shrugged. "But then, considering how little I get, they can't fire me. Slaves have to be sold, you know."

"I'd bid high for you."

"And set me free?" she asked lightly.

They stopped in a little clearing and faced each other. He gave her a long, speculative look. "I'm not sure," he said finally. "I don't think I'd want to."

"I'm afraid you'd have to." She moved her left hand so the emerald on it caught fire from the early-morning sun breaking through the clouds. "You see, I'm already owned."

What a stupid thing to have said! she thought, as his lips tightened in a sardonic smile and his eyes taunted her. "All bought and paid for?" he asked.

"That's insulting, Mr. . . . ." What *was* his name? Why wouldn't he tell her?

He looked directly at her with a frank, sincere expression. "I'm sorry. I shouldn't have said that. Please forgive me, Diane."

"How do you know my name?" she demanded sharply.

In a quiet voice, he said, "I'm Greg Kimball, Diane."

# - 2 -

THE SPOT IN which they stood seemed to become very still, like the eye of a hurricane. Quickly, almost desperately, as though her life depended on it, Diane searched her memory. Images flashed before her, stayed a second, then vanished like snapshots in an album, like the pages Vanessa, Lyle's sister, had turned. "That's Greg, our half-brother," she had said in her characteristically sniffy tone when Diane asked.

Greg, a lanky, dark-haired boy grinning impudently into the camera. Greg throwing a ball to kid-brother Lyle; posing unsmilingly, rebelliously, beside a prim young Vanessa; in mortarboard and academic gown at his college graduation. Greg on a ranch somewhere out West; in a Central American jungle; in a city skylined with mosques.

She scanned his face now, looking for a resemblance to Vanessa and Lyle. The finely etched nose and facial planes were the same, but he was dark whereas they were blue-eyed and fair. Then, too, he had a more rugged look than Lyle, and he was taller and more muscular. The gangling, tense-looking boy of the snapshots now had the self-assured air of a big man. Not much over thirty-five, he looked as though he had come to grips with himself and the world in a way many people never do.

Then the full import of his behavior exploded in her consciousness. This man who had pretended to be a stranger was her future brother-in-law!

A blaze of indignation raced through her. He must have known who she was from the moment she mentioned Holiday Homes and her family. Vanessa or Lyle would have told him about her links with Saint-Cast. Perhaps he had recognized her even sooner. It wouldn't have been unusual for Lyle to have sent his brother a picture of his prospective fiancée.

His remark about her having been bought and paid for became clear now. It had to have come from Vanessa, who made no secret of her suspicion that Diane was marrying Lyle for his money and that she had "tempted" him, as Vanessa put it in her old-fashioned way, so that he couldn't resist her.

Her eyes raking Greg with contempt, Diane said, "You knew I was here, of course."

He bowed his head slightly. "Of course."

"You must have been in a hurry," she said sardonically, "to make arrangements with Holiday Homes in one day."

Slowly, patiently, like a teacher explaining something to a young pupil, he said, "I'm an engineer, Diane. I build hydroelectric-power dams all over the world. I had just finished a job in Africa and decided to combine business with pleasure in France and Switzerland. Among other things, there's an international conference of engineers coming up in Geneva. I also want to look at several plants in this general area, particularly the Rance tidal-power station, which, as I'm sure you know, is only a few miles from here. At the same time, I wanted to enjoy as different a landscape and climate from Africa as I could get.

"I knew you were in Saint-Cast," he continued, "only because I had occasion to call Vanessa about some family business when I was in Paris. Since I planned to rent a house anyway and use it as a kind of home base while I traveled

around, what could be more natural than to rent one from
Holiday Homes?"

"What indeed?" Diane said automatically, her mind busy
with speculation about that phone conversation between Greg
and Vanessa. There would have been the hint that Lyle's
fiancée wasn't "quite their sort"; that it was obvious what
her interest in Lyle was, but Lyle, poor lamb, was so trusting
that he wouldn't listen to the slightest criticism of her.
Moreover, after the exhibition—so in character—that the
girl had made of herself in their own home town of Forestville, she, Vanessa, really couldn't see that James woman
ever fitting into the Kimball family.

Diane smiled wryly. Vanessa's ideas about life—and
men and women—were practically antediluvian. She was
a stereotype of what used to be called an old maid, jealous
of another woman's happiness. Not only had Diane not
"tempted" Lyle, but they hadn't even consummated their
engagement with anything other than a kiss and a ring. In
fact, the engagement was somewhat open-ended, since Lyle
had insisted before Diane left for Europe that if she met
someone else or changed her mind, she was to consider
herself free. And before Lyle, she had been faithful to Mike
until the day she became his widow, even though fidelity
was certainly not Mike's forte. Diane's smile gave way to
a sudden frown as she reflected that Vanessa's ideas were
not only ridiculous but could be dangerous, as well. Greg's
comment about her having been bought and paid for still
hurt.

She glanced through an opening in the pines toward the
smooth expanse of yellow sand and the green water beyond.
All her instincts drew her to the openness and freedom of
the beach. She would make some offhand remark about
having changed her mind about going to his house. Then
she would leave this stockade of soldierly straight trees and
run along the sea's edge again, letting the salt air and wind
wash away her anger.

But she didn't leave. She had learned many lessons in
life during her marriage to Mike. One was never to run

away, no matter how bad the situation. The other was to know herself, even when it hurt. And she had to admit, she was as curious about the man moving with easy strides beside her as she would be about a new planet in what she had thought was a completely mapped-out world. Besides, it was her duty to check on each house that was rented, and she hadn't yet done that with the Poilvet place.

So, doggedly, she placed one foot carefully in front of the other and walked along beside Greg Kimball until a turn in the forest path brought them to a clearing and the house he had rented. Built of white stone with a sloping roof of bluish-gray tiles set with dormer windows, it was typical of middle-class homes in Saint-Cast.

Diane had been in the house before, and as she stepped inside she recalled that the Poilvets were staunch Bretons with an interest in regional antiques. The kitchen table, a massive slab of dark oak, was flanked by two intricately carved settles. Rows of Quimper ware, glazed pottery dishes decorated with blue and white peasant figures, were arranged in wooden racks on the walls and over the mantel of an open fireplace. In the next room, a grandfather clock stood in a corner; a huge armoire, decoratively carved and mellowed with age to a golden patina, occupied one wall; and a piece of furniture that looked like a combination wooden cupboard and bench lined another.

"I've already learned enough Breton from a booklet I picked up to know that the name on the front of the house, *Ti Gwenn,* means 'white house.' I think I've mastered the hot-water heater. But what the hell is that thing?" Greg asked, pointing to the freestanding cupboard.

"It's called a *lit clos,*" Diane explained. "Literally, a 'closed bed.' It's what the people of Brittany formerly used for sleeping. A cupboard-bed gave them privacy when they all slept in one room; it protected the children from farm animals that might wander into the house when the family was out in the fields; and the mother could put the cradle on the bench and rock her baby from inside. It was really quite handy."

Diane opened the hand-carved chestnut panels and looked in at the red feather bed and goosedown pillow covered with an embroidered white linen pillowcase. She sniffed appreciatively at the fresh, sunny smell of linens dried outdoors.

Greg stepped closer to her. She could feel his warm breath on her cheek as he, too, looked inside. A long, muscular thigh brushed against hers. A honey-sweet ripple of excitement surged up inside her. She heard her own quick intake of breath and hurriedly withdrew her head and stepped back. As she did so, they touched again. She could feel a tremor pass through Greg's powerful male body. He flinched, then put out his hand to her. But whether his purpose was to hold her or to ward her off, Diane didn't know. For a long moment they stood looking at each other, flushed and confused by the electric current that had so obviously passed between them.

"I thought people were smaller in those days," he said gruffly. "This thing's big enough even for me."

Quickly, nervously, Diane said, "You're right, people were smaller. But often several people at a time slept in these beds. Maybe this one was made extra large for that purpose." She lifted the seat of the bench. "And see, they put their clothes in here," she continued brightly. Too brightly, she told herself with a grimace. She took a step toward the door and said, "I'd like to check out the house if you don't mind. I'm supposed to. Then I'll be going. I'm afraid I won't have time for coffee after all."

"Still mad at me for that crack I made earlier, Diane?" His eyes studied her keenly.

"Not at all. It was perfectly natural on your part. That's what Vanessa thinks, that I'm marrying Lyle for the Kimball money."

"And you believe I get my ideas from Vanessa?" His tone had turned hard and his dark eyes were as opaque as volcanic rock. Put like that, it did seem ridiculous to believe that this virile, sophisticated man could be influenced by a rigidly snobbish spinster like Vanessa. Then he relaxed, and his expression softened. "Look, it was a stupid remark, a smart-ass answer to what, don't forget, you started—all that joking around about being a slave and being owned."

"So it was *my* fault then," she said hotly.

He looked at her admiringly without answering for a moment, and she could feel her face flame up to the roots of her hair.

"You know, you're gorgeous when you get mad," he finally said. "It's too bad for his sake that Lyle isn't a more provoking man."

"Like you, I suppose."

He grinned. "With me, you'd be Miss America every day of the week."

"I'm leaving, Greg," she said coldly. "The house looks perfectly all right to me. If any problems arise, you can always call me."

"I'll tell Hilary Pentwhistle you didn't inspect it."

"You forget, I can't be fired."

"Only sold; I know."

They were back to square one. They looked at each other and burst into laughter.

"Oh, no," Diane said. "Not again."

Greg extended a hand toward her. "Come on, let's make up and be friends."

The grip of his long, supple fingers sent a disturbing jolt of excitement through Diane. She withdrew her hand, smiling to make up for her abruptness. "Where's that coffee?" she asked.

A broad grin spread across his face. "Coming right up."

She followed Greg into the kitchen and watched his capable-looking sun-browned hands deftly measure coffee and water into a speckled gray and white pot. She cut the bread, placed sweet Normandy butter and apricot preserves on the table, and meticulously portioned out the remaining *pain au chocolat*.

When they had sat down opposite each other, elbows on the table, large breakfast cups of whitish-brown *café au lait* in front of them, Greg said, "I'm going to the Rance power station today. I'm sure you've seen it, but not with a trained hot-shot engineer. Want to go with me and I'll show you how it works?"

Diane shrugged. "I've seen it from a distance on my way to Saint-Malo."

"And you never stopped to look at it—the first hydro-electric plant in the world to use tidal energy?" His voice rang with disbelief.

Diane turned away to hide a smile. He was so intense about that Rance station! "I'm not all bad," she said with mock humility. "I don't cheat on my income tax or steal library books."

But he was still shaking his head and looking at her sternly. "I just can't believe it. One of the greatest engineering marvels of our time, and you wouldn't even stop at the visitors' center. Well, how about this afternoon?"

"I'm afraid I have an appointment." It was the truth, but it sounded like an excuse even to her.

His sable eyes gleamed as if he were amused by her seeming lie. "That's okay, we'll do it another time. I'm going to be studying the plant for quite a while. I have a contract in the States to build minihydros now—that is, small localized dams and power plants—but I'm interested in tidal power for its energy-saving potential." He flashed an amiable grin at her. "I didn't mean to hit the roof about the Rance project. I'm just a nut about hydro power. But I suppose Lyle and Vanessa have already told you that."

As a matter of fact, they hadn't, Diane reflected. They had never really said much about their half-brother Greg. Most of the stories had been about how Vanessa had left college after their parents' death to make a home for Lyle, how she had turned down at least one offer of marriage for the same reason, and how the two of them together had taken over the family construction business and made it even more profitable than it had been before.

More comfortable with Greg now, Diane shook her head slowly in an invitation for him to tell her about himself.

"Ah, well, maybe they didn't," he said. His tone was reflective, and he took a long sip of coffee as if carefully choosing his words. "I wasn't home that much, and we weren't very close. Their mother never liked me because I was the product of a youthful indiscretion on my dad's part. In plain English, he wasn't married to my mother, who died soon after I was born. I think Louise—that was my stepmother's name—suspected Dad married her just to give me a home. When I was old enough, she shipped me off to boarding school. I honestly think she believed that as an illegitimate child I'd be a bad influence on her children." He paused a moment. "I tried to get better acquainted with Lyle and Vanessa later, when Dad and Louise were killed in his Cessna, but without much success. Lyle and I had been apart too long for any brotherly intimacy, and Vanessa had absorbed her mother's ideas about me. I mean, no way would I ever make it into Forestville's social register. So, after a few years of fulfilling the family prophecy about me by sowing the usual wild oats, I broke loose from my hangups and went to engineering school. Then I used my inheritance to start my own company."

He got up then, took the coffee pot from the gas stove, and poured more of the thick, dark liquid into her cup.

"It's the coffee you eat with a spoon," he said, smiling.

She raised a skeptical eyebrow at the brimming cup. "You didn't ask if I wanted more."

"I plan to keep you here, a prisoner of caffeine, so I can find out what dire fate made you a singing courier in Saint-Cast."

Diane laughed joyously in a series of musical notes. "Don't knock it! I actually did that for a while back in the States—delivering singing telegrams at birthday parties—as well as belting out operatic numbers in an Italian restaurant in Chicago, modeling, and giving voice and piano lessons." All of these endeavors, Diane reflected, had been openly disapproved of by Vanessa on the grounds of poor taste, poor payment, and, therefore, lack of class.

She didn't think it necessary to mention that the modeling had been of lingerie. It had been as impersonal as demonstrating steel pipe, but Vanessa had greeted Diane's frankness with a horrified "You won't ever let anyone in Forestville know, will you, dear?" Diane thought it might be wise to enlarge the borders of Forestville to include Greg Kimball, but not because he'd be horrified. On the contrary, from the way he was looking at the graceful swoop of her neck down to her well-set shoulders and the shapely outline of her breasts under the thin cotton shirt she wore beneath her jogging suit, she thought he'd be delighted.

"Sounds as though you needed money," he drawled.

"I did. I worked my way through college, as well as rehearsing and appearing in every opera the music department staged."

"So you're an opera singer?" Greg said, his eyes shining with interest.

"Not really." Diane flushed and lowered her head. "I gave up trying when I married." She laughed then, a wry little laugh at herself. "Doesn't sound very liberated, does it? But it wouldn't have been possible—the hard work and training, the long separations." She stammered a little under his piercing gaze. "I was a bride... I wanted to do what was good for my husband... things that would help him in his career. That meant the social scene—entertaining, charity work, membership in cultural organizations. But when Mike—my husband—died, I decided to try for an operatic career again."

"How are you going to sing in an opera, stuck in a little resort town in Brittany?"

"Many young American singers start out in Europe because there are more opera companies here. I took this job with Holiday Homes with the understanding that I would be able to take time off in August and go to Nice to audition with the Opera Company of the Riviera. A friend of mine named Yann Duhamel is going to pinch-hit for me while I'm gone. I'll give you his phone number before I leave."

He flicked his eyes over the large, square green stone on her left hand. "Lyle doesn't mind the separation?"

"He expects to be coming to Brittany to look at some land. He and Vanessa are interested in building tract homes in Europe, particularly here in France."

"I see. But suppose this Opera Company of the Riviera gives you a contract? I believe they're usually for a year. Lyle can't take that much time away from the firm. Will he be able to wait?" His eyes, mocking now, roved insolently over the curves of her generous mouth and full, well-formed breasts. "*I* couldn't." He laughed and looked at her in a way that was humorously suggestive.

"I don't see how Lyle's waiting concerns *you,*" she snapped.

It concerns *me,* though, she thought ruefully. It was the one small cloud she could see on the horizon when she thought of her forthcoming marriage. Lyle was one of the twin pillars of Forestville society; the other Corinthian being his sister Vanessa. As understanding as Lyle was of Diane's need to succeed as a singer, and as undemanding a husband as he gave every promise of being, would he be able to withstand the tongue-wagging that a long separation from his bride would cause? Then Diane shrugged off her concern. For all Lyle's gentleness, he was strong underneath. He had given evidence of that during Mike's long illness when he had overridden the board of directors so that Mike would get his full pay as sales manager. What was more, Lyle had bolstered Diane's courage almost daily as she watched her husband slowly lose his struggle against leukemia. Besides, their love wasn't the fierce, overwhelming kind that could brook no delay in its fulfillment. It was a tender, affectionate emotion, a limpid pool that lapped gently at their lives—not a riptide of passion.

Greg's brown eyes sparkled with suppressed amusement. "Vanessa seems to think your engagement to Lyle concerns *her.*"

"I suppose she told you about my singing Rosalinde in the Forestville Operetta Company's production of *Die Fledermaus* last month." Diane's voice shook with injured pride. "She was terribly upset about my costumes, which were pretty low-cut, I'll admit, but that's what the role calls for, particularly in the second act, where there's a lot of business about Rosalinde's husband trying to get his watch away from her after she hides it in her décolletage. I tried to explain that to Vanessa, but she hit the ceiling anyway. I don't know what bothered her more—the fact that I had disgraced Lyle and her before Forestville high society or had revealed myself for what she thought I really was—a public performer of low morals who was leading her brother astray. Anyway, she accused me of manipulating Lyle into a marriage that would elevate me to the fortune and social position of the Kimballs but do nothing for Lyle except satisfy his short-lived sensual desires. Then she called me a temptress. It was all perfectly ridiculous, and she made a half-hearted apology afterward, but even so . . ."

"I trust you fought back?"

The memory of Vanessa's face, paper-white with hate, the small blue eyes coldly self-righteous as she hurled the epithet *temptress* at her, returned, and Diane answered ruefully, "Not very hard, I'm afraid."

Greg's glance was shrewdly speculative. "But surely Lyle came to your defense."

"Lyle was away on a business trip at the time. *I* certainly wouldn't stoop to telling him. Whether Vanessa did, I don't know or care." She shrugged. "Lyle never said anything to me about it. But believe me, I was very glad to get away from Forestville and come to Saint-Cast."

With a quick, impulsive motion, he put his hand out and laid it on hers. "I'm sorry we Kimballs have given you such a hard time."

The feel of his rough, outdoors skin on her soft hand made her acutely aware of his potent masculinity. She noticed the dark hair on his arm and his heavy, wide wristbone. She was seized by an irrational impulse to put her own long, smooth fingers around his wrist, to measure it, in a sense.

"Only Vanessa," she reminded him, pulling her hand away. And possibly you, she thought. She stood up, and Greg stood, too. Her gray, almond-shaped eyes searched his warm brown ones, looking for an answer to the way she felt—flushed and quick and excited, as though her system were being charged with adrenaline. She had felt that way when she met Mike and it had lasted for the first year of their marriage, until she made the discoveries that convulsed her life into chaos. An 8.2 Richter-scale earthquake, that's what her marriage had become when she finally put it all together—the presents Mike gave her for no good reason, the wrong-number calls when he jumped to answer the phone, the faint aura of a perfume she never used, even the change in his lovemaking. He had been too smart, or too experienced, for the obvious—lipstick smears on his collar, dark hairs on his shoulder.

With practiced self-discipline, Diane pulled herself away from the familiar dead-end street her thoughts were taking her on. So far as Greg was concerned, it was all academic anyway. Sitting together at a Kimball family Thanksgiving dinner would be all the involvement she and Lyle's half-brother would ever have.

Starting for the door, she said with a crisp, professional smile, "Everything seems to be in good shape, but feel free to call me if you have any problems. That's my job."

His dark eyes bright with amusement, he looked down at her as she stood with her hand on the doorknob. "Remember, we have a hot date for the Rance power plant."

She exploded into laughter, the idea of having a good time at a hydroelectric plant seeming inexpressibly funny.

Greg pretended to be hurt. "I'll bet you don't laugh at Lyle like that."

Even though he was joking, his statement jolted Diane. It was true; she and Lyle didn't laugh with each other. In fact, they didn't laugh at anything much, together.

Suddenly subdued, she said soberly, "I'll think about it—the trip to the power plant."

"Do you always have to plan ahead, have everything under control, Diane?"

"Yes," she snapped, annoyed at his putting her on the defensive. "I find I make fewer mistakes that way."

"Small risks, small gains. It doesn't add up to much of a life, does it?" he mused aloud.

"Maybe not, but it adds up to my life." She spoke rapidly, her eyes flashing with anger.

"And Lyle's, too."

"Oh, so that's it. You don't think I'm the right woman for your brother."

His sardonic eyes looked deep and straight into hers. "Just the opposite. I'm not sure he's the man for you."

"And who's asking *you*—a man who's an outcast from his own family?" It was hitting below the belt, but Diane didn't care. He had driven her to it with his probing and his insults and interference.

"Aren't we both outcasts, Diane?"

With an annoyed flick of her wrist, she turned the door handle and walked out.

# - 3 -

HER TANTE YVONNE'S house was at the opposite end of the crescent-shaped bay. Diane chose the forest path instead of the beach, because it was shorter. In her present mood, she wanted to put the greatest possible distance between Greg Kimball and herself in the shortest possible time. She walked quickly, oblivious to both the slippery path and the smell of the sea-kissed pines. She could have been in a cement tunnel for all the impact the outside world was having on her.

The things Greg had said to her kept going round and round in her mind like clothes in one of those washing machines with a porthole in the door where you could watch shirts go flying by—arms flung out as if for help—and blue jeans stiff as cowpokes' legs. That's what she had been doing when she met Mike, Diane mused—watching her weekly wash in a laundromat near her apartment building. She had stayed up the night before studying for an exam in an evening class in advanced harmony and had worked all day as cashier at a discount-record store. Exhausted and half-hypnotized from watching her clothes go around and around, she had fallen asleep. When she woke up, her washing machine was empty. She panicked, thinking someone had taken her clothes, but Mike came over to her and said he had put them in the dryer. He invited her out for coffee while the clothes were drying, and they had started dating immediately. Looking back, it seemed to Diane that she had fallen in love with Mike right away, in that little all-night white-tiled coffee shop. He was a salesman for Kimball Construction and had a salesman's personality—outgoing, personable, and confident—whereas Diane was unsure of everything but her looks. Without money or social status, with a B. A. in music but no skill except singing—and that was yet to be tested—at twenty-one she felt unrooted and apprehensive about her future.

In contrast, Mike's confidence seemed godlike. She loved being with him. He buoyed her up, made her laugh, loved her at a time when she needed love. They went together only two months before they decided to get married, on the day that Lyle Kimball told Mike he had a future with the company and could expect to be made sales manager in the not-too-distant future. After they were married, they laughed about their laundromat romance. Friends teased her about going from folding towels to folding diapers. But it hadn't worked out that way. When she found out about Mike's philandering, she began to plan a divorce, not a baby. Then he had gotten sick with what turned out to be leukemia. She wouldn't leave him, but neither was it the time to have a child.

If Greg thought she was overly careful and controlling, too bad—*tant pis,* as the French said. You can't step twice in the same stream, and at twenty-eight her days of careless rapture were over. She had loved Mike passionately and he had betrayed her—not once, but countless times. It was in the very nature of men to seek sexual variety, Mike had said; well, so be it. At least she would never again pay for a husband's extramarital excitement with a broken heart. If Lyle wanted to roam after they were married, there'd be no hot, wrenching tears cried silently into a pillow. Dear as

Lyle was to her, neither he nor any other man would be her all in all as Mike had been. What's more, she now had a career to ensure her emotional independence.

She had certainly run the emotional gamut in the last few hours, Diane thought with a wry laugh. In that short time span, Greg Kimball had made her laugh, infuriated her, and even, she had to admit, excited her a little.

When she walked through the front door, Diane looked at her aunt's house with new eyes. It was as different from the Poilvet place as Paris was from Brittany. No dark, massive armoires and cupboard-beds here. Yvonne Lannec had furnished her house with rattan, blond woods, bright cushions, and woven rugs as vivid as tropical islands. And on the walls were none of the usual scenes of Brittany—castles and lighthouses and the craggy coast. Instead, there were old French theater posters—clowns and masked harlequins and Maurice Chevalier's yellow straw hat with a smile and a bow tie beneath it.

None of the furniture was expensive. In fact, much of it had been picked up by Tante Yvonne at the famous Clignancourt flea market in the north section of Paris, on Saturday mornings, when the expert bargain searchers went. Yvonne Lannec wasn't wealthy. She worked as a dressmaker for a small fashion house in Paris and lived in a modest apartment on a narrow old street off Boulevard Raspail. The house in Saint-Cast was an inheritance, shared with her sister, Diane's mother, until the latter's death five years before.

When she didn't use the place herself during the annual August exodus of Parisians from their city, Yvonne often gave it to Holiday Homes to rent for her. It was through her aunt's influence that Diane got the summer job she needed. Because she was bilingual in French and English and knew Saint-Cast and the area around it intimately from summers spent there as a young girl, Diane was ideally suited to help the foreign clients of Holiday Homes.

Yvonne had been delighted when her niece got the temporary job. Through necessity, the older woman, like the younger, knew the value of a franc, or dollar, earned.

And although she had never married, how different Tante Yvonne was from Vanessa Kimball, Diane thought. She had spread her warm affections among members of her family and her host of friends, most of whom had strange-sounding nicknames like Loulou and Bobo and Minou and were unconventional members of the artistic set that frequented the cafés of the Left Bank.

Diane's eyes glowed softly when she thought of Paris. She loved the city and had promised herself a few days there on the way back to Saint-Cast from the Riviera. She would stay at Tante Yvonne's apartment and air the place out a bit, and at her aunt's request make sure Madame Bertin, the *concièrge*, was watering the geraniums in the window regularly as she had promised she would.

There was no theater or opera in Paris in August, but there would be recitals and, in the city's famous churches, chamber music. The museums would be open, including the Beaubourg with its nonstop carnival of trained dog acts, mimes, jugglers, sword-swallowers, and musicians on the huge plaza in front. The summer sales of clothing would still be on. And even if one did nothing purposeful, Paris was the best city in which to do it. What could be more delightful than to stroll on the Champs-Elysées, sit in a café and watch people go by, or browse at the bookstalls along the Seine?

With a start, Diane remembered that her guests would be arriving at the house in a very short while. Yann Duhamel had promised to come with some fellow musicians and play Breton songs for her to record. Yann was a school teacher whose high color and sturdy build revealed the farm boy he once had been. He was one of a group who met to speak Breton, one of the Celtic languages, and to play the traditional musical instruments. Diane and Yann had become friends during the summers she had spent in Saint-Cast visiting her aunt. She had shared his interest in Breton songs then, and in time widened that interest to include other folk music. She had taken courses in ethnomusicology in college and started collecting recordings of songs; a friend had given her one of Chinese lute music, and Diane herself had recorded some southern Appalachian ballads. But opera was her first love; folk music just a hobby.

Diane went into the living room and plumped up a pillow here and there. Then, deciding that she'd leave it to Yann and his friends to arrange the furniture as they wanted it, she turned and left. Her glance fell on the old-fashioned black telephone in the hall, and into her mind flashed a picture of the Poilvet house and Greg Kimball. With a mild sense of horror, she realized what she was doing. Thinking of him! Wondering if he'd call!

She moved uneasily, superstitiously, away from the phone. Just looking at it might make it ring. But the damage had already been done. With the harsh jangle that set her teeth on edge every time, it rang, and with a pounding heart, she picked it up.

"Diane, this is Yann. We're ready to come over right now, but first I want to prepare you for a little surprise."

Relief at hearing her friend's voice instead of Greg Kimball's made Diane laugh and ask in a lilting tone, "How can it be a surprise if you tell me about it, Yann?"

"Ah, you French-Americans from Forestville, Iowa, how logical you are."

"Forestville, Illinois, Yann."

"Wherever, as they say in your country. Now to get to the point, do you remember Guy Kerbellec?"

"What a question! Of course I do. Guy and Nadia and you were my closest friends when I used to come to Saint-Cast."

Yann chuckled. "Well, Guy's become a famous Celtic bard, and he and Nadia are coming today."

"Celtic bard! You must be kidding."

"Don't laugh; he's doing very well. He started as a Breton folk singer like so many of us. Then he got the brilliant idea to enlarge his scope and sing Celtic—not just Breton—songs and accompany himself on an ancient harp. Now he travels to Ireland and other parts of the British Isles, as well as Brittany and Paris. He draws big crowds everywhere and is becoming very rich. So you see, he is doing you a great honor by coming to your home." Behind Yann's clear, precise French was a suggestion of suppressed laughter.

"All right, I feel properly honored. But why—"

"Why did I call? Oh, I just thought you'd appreciate advance notice that the Kerbellecs were coming. See you soon."

With that, Yann hung up. And with a shrug and a laugh, Diane put the phone down. In a hurry now, she showered quickly and changed into a pair of white clam diggers and a T-shirt with broad daffodil-yellow and white stripes. Then she brushed her red-gold hair vigorously. Naturally curly, it had a tendency to become frizzy in the damp sea air. It was so luxuriantly thick that Diane sometimes had the feeling she was taming a wild beast when she brushed it. Other times she acknowledged without vanity that her hair was truly her "crowning glory." Its color ran the gamut of gold and red shades, and it tumbled around her face and onto her shoulders in burnished waves, setting off her fine translucent skin and clear gray eyes.

Because Saint-Cast was a family resort and not a high-style watering hole like Deauville, Diane wore little makeup during the day. A sunscreen was essential even in the comparatively mild northern sun, but once she had acquired a slight tan, a copper-toned lipstick was the only cosmetic she needed. She had just finished applying it when the doorbell rang.

Yann and someone she remembered as Marc stood on the threshold, but it was the third man who drew her attention. He was tall and well-built, with dark, wavy hair that fell to his shoulders, framing a pleasant, open face and the same sea-gray Breton eyes Diane had. A gold chain that dangled down the front of a soft, open-necked white shirt ended in a large circular pendant bearing the interlocking scrolls characteristic of Celtic art. He carried a graceful-looking small harp painted green and gold with entwined gold shamrocks along the frame.

Diane shifted her gaze to the petite brunette at Guy's side, who was as physically unlike her brother as any siblings could be. Diane didn't know which of the two people beaming at her to embrace first, so with a small cry of happiness she threw her arms wide around both.

"I can't believe it! It's so good to see you! You look wonderful, both of you. Nadia, you are so *chic!* Come in and let me look at you."

Diane's voice, a high soprano when she spoke French, blended with the joyous, excited sounds of her friends. They all spilled, rather than walked, into the house, then stood fondly looking at each other again.

"You're as lovely as ever, Diane," Guy said, "and you are to be married, I hear."

"Yes, and I'm dying to have my fiancé—his name is Lyle—meet you and Nadia. I've told him so much about both of you." Diane smiled warmly at the pair. "I would have known Guy anywhere, even with the long hair, but you, Nadia, you are so quintessentially Paris with that geometric cut and gamine figure."

The girl laughed. "I know, I was a Breton dumpling the last time you saw me."

"And you, Guy," Diane said softly. "Yann has told me what a success you've become."

"Yes, you know I always liked the old Breton songs; all of us did. Well, I decided to make them better known. To my surprise, I found many people wanted to hear them, and I became popular." His gray eyes twinkled. "See, Diane, you should have said yes when I asked you to sing with me in those cellar clubs in Rennes."

Diane chuckled. "I probably would have, except that I made the mistake of telling Tante Yvonne. She was furious. 'What! Sing in some smoky little *cave* in a provincial capital? Your mother has better ideas for you than *that*, my girl. She wants to see you in the Paris opera house.'"

"And you may make it, eh, Diane? I understand you're trying out for the Riviera company."

A discreet cough from Yann reminded Diane that the

group had come to record songs. Putting her hand on Guy's arm, she said, "I want to tell you about it, Guy, and hear all about what you've been doing since we lost track of each other, but perhaps we'd better get started on the music."

Diane ushered everyone into the living room, saying, "This room has the best acoustics. I use it as my practice room for that reason, and because it has a piano. But are you sure you wouldn't like some coffee and cake before we begin?"

She had baked a Breton butter cake the day before. It was a simple cake made with almost equal quantities of flour, butter and sugar; egg yolks; and a little baking powder. Diane herself liked it for its rich buttery taste.

"Do you mind if we do our songs first?" Guy said. "I promised to sing tonight at the Festival of the Saint-Jean, and I would like to rest my voice for as long as possible between now and then."

Yann made some remark about really getting started, and they all moved about, arranging furniture and music stands and the instruments they had brought. These were the *biniou*, the Breton bagpipe, smaller and somewhat different from the Highland pipes; the *bombarde*, a kind of oboe usually played in duets with the *biniou;* an accordion; and Guy's harp.

The songs the group played were those of a people who were both rural and seafaring, peasants and fishermen. They were songs of the thousand and one events of the working day, tragedies at sea, loved ones lost, and love both returned and unrequited.

Diane knew most, if not all, of them. They were the songs of her mother's childhood before she left France to marry the American soldier with whom she had fallen in love. Her mother had played them on the piano and taught Diane to sing them, insisting, because she herself had a good voice and knew music, that Diane do so correctly and well.

After the group had performed several songs, Marc said, "Why don't you sing for us now, Diane?"

"No, really," she objected, "I'd rather not. It's *your* music I want on my tapes."

"Turn about is fair play," Marc insisted firmly.

"All right then," she answered. "What would you like to hear?"

"'The Morning Kiss,'" Marc said softly.

"I don't know it in Breton."

"Then sing it in French," Guy said. "It's a beautiful song in any language."

So, with just the oboe as accompaniment, Diane sang about the happiness of two lovers who wake up side by side and kiss on a May morning. As she sang, her initial reluctance yielded to the joyful sensuousness of the song. She could feel the freshness of the dawn wind and the flower-sweet air, and see the lovers as they tenderly exchanged their first kiss of the day.

It was a sentimental song, but poignant, too. It seemed to Diane to capture the essence of romantic love, not only the joy but also the yearning, when at the end the lovers wonder if their ecstasy will last.

It hadn't with Mike, she reflected. But she still had Lyle's love, warm and protective of her as . . . what? . . . a security blanket? Diane hurriedly pushed the troublesome thought out of her mind. Her glance drifted to the door.

She was startled to see Greg there, holding her *Herald Tribune* up in silent explanation of why he had come. The look on his face mesmerized her.

Admiration was part of it, as his eyes roved over her strong shoulders, the firm globes of her breasts proudly outlined by the cotton shirt, and her graceful, womanly hips. But Diane had long ago learned to write off men's glances as irrelevant to her own idea of herself. Her beauty had only professional importance to her. Reddish-gold hair and gray eyes fringed with sooty lashes were an unusual combination, and therefore, like her full-bodied, shapely figure, an asset on the operatic stage.

There was something else in Greg's expression that bothered Diane even more than the frank sensual appreciation she saw there. It was a fierce concentration that seemed intent on knowing the woman Diane James was. At the same time, a slight flaring of the aristocratic Kimball nostrils and a latent smoldering in the dark non-Kimball eyes signaled a challenge that sent a provocative tremor through her.

She regretted having let herself go in the song. She wouldn't have, she thought, if she had known Greg was there. On the other hand, it would have been impossible for her to render so hauntingly sensuous a melody mechanically. Tossing her head, she looked away from Greg and responded kindly to the compliments of her friends.

Then, in one long step, Greg was at her side. "You forgot your paper. I knocked, but no one heard."

He said nothing about her performance. And to her surprise, because she never fished for compliments, Diane heard herself asking, "Didn't you like the song? Or was it the singer?"

"Frankly, I found both too beautiful for comment." The quiet sincerity in his voice moved her. She studied his face a moment, noticing again how different he was from Lyle. So much darker, his skin so weather-bronzed, he might have been a gypsy child taken into the family.

Then, as though embarrassed by this emotional response, Greg nodded toward Guy Kerbellec and said dryly, "Who's the druid?"

His sarcasm broke the spell between them. Diane answered sharply, "His name's Guy Kerbellec and he's a very accomplished folk singer, as well as an old friend of mine. Come," she continued more graciously, "I'll introduce you to everyone."

After Greg had been welcomed by the group, Yann and the others called for Diane to sing something from her operatic repertoire. Diane disliked giving the appearance of wanting to be coaxed, so without further ado she joined Yann at the piano. Because she had been practicing Gilda's famous "Caro nome" aria from *Rigoletto* and the score was still on the music stand, she told Yann she would sing that.

The song, which expressed the feelings of a young girl experiencing the wonderment of love for the first time, was a beautiful one, and Diane sang it with feeling. When she had finished, she politely acknowledged the applause of her friends, but her eyes were on Nadia. The young woman had a rapt look on her face. Did she have a lover, or was she only wishing for one?

Nadine, or Nadia as they all called her, had been the little sister tagging along when Diane and Guy and the others had gone swimming in the cold green water of the bay or searched the cliffs for birds' nests in those idyllic summers of Diane's youth. Because of the age difference between them, Diane had not been very close to Nadia. Guy and Diane, on the other hand, had been inseparable. Yet the friendship she and Guy enjoyed had always remained just that, never taking on the tinge of a romantic interest.

Quietly, so as not to interrupt the conversation that had started, Diane went into the kitchen. She prepared the coffee and was slicing the cake when Guy entered. He put his hand on her shoulder and looked down at what she was doing.

"Why don't you come to the Saint-Jean with Nadia and me tonight?" he said. "I have to sing only two or three songs; then we can spend the rest of the evening together."

Before she could answer, Greg's deep baritone filled the kitchen. "Too bad, friend, but Diane's promised to go to the Saint-Jean with me."

Guy dropped his hand and turned around, at the same time that Diane opened her mouth to repudiate Greg's statement. But with a quick movement, Greg put the plate of sliced cake in Guy's hand and said, "Here, let's help Diane. You serve this and I'll bring in the coffee." He gave Guy a slight shove toward the door, and with a dazed look in his eyes, Guy carried the cake out of the kitchen.

"That wasn't very nice," Diane said.

"Nice guys don't get to go to the Saint-Jean with the girl of their dreams. What the hell *is* the Saint-Jean, by the way?"

"Suppose I said it was a concert put on by the Society

of Ancient Instruments and Decrepit Players?" Diane said playfully.

"I'd go anyway." He paused. "If you were going."

Her heart leaped up at his suggestive tone, but she kept her gray-eyed gaze steady as she looked at him. She had no desire to flirt with Lyle's brother. "Fortunately, it isn't," she said. "The Saint-Jean is the feast day of Saint John the Baptist. But actually it's a fifteen-hundred-year-old summer-solstice celebration that was Christianized to a saint's day. It's celebrated by the Bretons in a unique way. And I didn't exactly hear myself accepting your invitation."

"You have to accept it now. I told your druid friend we were going."

"I told you once before he's not a druid," Diane retorted.

"But he *is* your friend."

Diane turned and faced him squarely. "Checking up for Lyle?"

"No," he said softly, "I'm working on my own time now." He reached for the tray of coffee things. "Want me to carry these in?"

The afternoon passed pleasantly in flurries of conversation carried on in both French and English. Since England was just across the Channel from Brittany, Yann and his friends spoke English with varying degrees of ease. And Greg's French, while not as fluent as Diane's, was adequate.

At first the conversation was about music, with many different crosscurrents of talk going on at the same time. But when Greg started talking about building dams in far-off places in the world, he had everyone's attention. He spoke well and had that rare quality of being able to describe technical subjects clearly in lay terms.

"And you and your fellow engineers were without women all that time?" Marc asked after Greg had described setting up camp in a remote region.

"As a matter of fact, no. When conditions weren't too tough, our wives accompanied us."

*Our* wives? *He was married!* His remark when they first

met about being a bachelor had been a lie. Diane was shocked at the quick stab of disappointment she felt. After all, what was Greg Kimball's marital status to her?

"Then I compliment you on your wife, Greg," Yann said quietly. "That would take a great deal of dedication and love—to live in such conditions."

"I'm afraid my wife didn't have that kind of dedication . . . or love," Greg answered dryly. "She did go on a project with me once, but she couldn't stand the rather primitive facilities and left as soon as she could. And staying home alone for long stretches of time didn't work out for her, either. I was willing to keep trying, even to go into another line of engineering, but by then she had found another man and asked for a divorce." Greg said all this in a flat, emotionless tone, but the way he compressed his lips gave Diane the idea that he had been badly hurt at the time.

"It's hard to tell about women," Guy said with a typical Gallic shrug. "Sometimes you find a good one right away and sometimes you never do."

"I've heard just the opposite," Diane said with a laugh. "In my country, there's a saying, 'A good man's hard to find.' "

"But of course, *chérie*," Guy answered. "That's why you should come to France to shop." With that, he bent his lips to her arm and ran kisses along it in exaggerated mockery of a French movie lover.

Diane tittered, but catching a glimpse of Greg's expression she could see he wasn't amused.

When Diane's friends left with handshakes and promises to see each other that night at the Saint-Jean, Greg stayed behind.

"You have a nice voice," he said. "But I suppose Lyle's already told you that."

Diane laughed. "Lyle doesn't know beans about opera. He thinks the Flying Dutchman was a pilot for KLM. But he's very supportive," she added quickly.

A wicked grin lit his face. "Blind love is stupid love.

Wouldn't you rather be loved by a man who knew you . . . thoroughly?"

"I'm satisfied with the love I'm receiving now," she said stubbornly.

"Are you, Diane?"

His tone was as darkly seductive as his eyes. Diane knew the pull of her desire for him. She felt as she had when she was a child, digging her toes into the wet sand so the dangerous undertow wouldn't pull her out to sea. But she wasn't a child any longer.

"Are you?" he repeated, searching her eyes with his. He put his finger on her lower lip and with slow deliberation traced its full, pouting curve. The effect on her was hypnotic. She shut her eyes and swayed a little with the intimacy of the gesture and the drawn-out, delicious tingling sensation it produced.

She continued to stand like that, as if in an erotic trance, while he caressed her cheek and traced her bones with the tips of his fingers. It was as though he was trying to learn who she was through her face alone. Then his hands dropped to her shoulders. He pulled her in to him and, pliant as a willow, she moved with him. She opened her eyes and glanced up into his deeply tanned face and onyx-dark eyes, and at the firm mouth that was descending toward hers. An unexpected stab of longing pierced her whole body. She wanted that kiss more than anything, and that, she thought in a brief flash of irony, made it without question the one kiss she couldn't have. So she backed away before their bodies could touch and, reaching up, put her hands on his and took them from her shoulders. She held them a moment as though she might just possibly place them again where they had been. Then she dropped them abruptly and said, "I'm engaged to your brother, Greg. That's something we both have to respect."

"You don't love him, Diane. You couldn't respond to me as you do if you really loved Lyle."

She moved away from him; then turned and faced him,

arms folded defensively across her breasts. "You're wrong, Greg. I do love Lyle. Oh, maybe not passionately." She hesitated. "Maybe not in the sense of *wanting* him terribly, as I might *want* other men." She emphasized *want* each time, putting an inflection of amusement in her voice, as though belittling the feeling. "But enough to marry him, and he loves me in pretty much the same way. There are marriages based on affection and friendship, you know. Successful marriages. Lyle and I came to know each other very well while my husband was sick. It wasn't only that, as Mike's boss, he helped us financially. He also gave us moral support. He visited Mike and shared the problems of the sales department with him, as though Mike were still a valued employee. He let me cry on his shoulder. He took me out to eat when I was so tired from taking care of Mike that I'd fall asleep on the couch, unable even to fix supper for myself. Lyle and I talked about ourselves, about our feelings, about life . . . and death. After Mike died, it seemed the most natural thing in the world for the two of us to decide to marry."

"That isn't love, Diane. You and Lyle invested yourselves in Mike and his illness. Your world probably shrank to each other and Mike. Then, when you no longer had Mike, you still had each other. You mistook a special kind of closeness for love. You're not being fair to yourself." He paused. "Or Lyle."

For a long minute Diane just stood there, staring at him, her hands balled up into fists. She wanted to scream "Get out!" at him like a hysterical heroine in an old movie. She wanted to tell him that she had had enough of truth. She had faced up to it too often with Mike, and it had worn her out.

But she controlled herself and said patiently, "I'm not jaded with life, Greg. I don't need thrills or infatuation in a relationship. I love the man I'm engaged to marry, and he loves me. We have a straightforward relationship. I also have a career that's very important to me, a career I intend to follow when I'm married." She walked toward the door in a gesture of dismissal. "If you pick me up at six, we'll have plenty of time for the festival. Yann and the others should be there by then, too."

"There's no safety in numbers, Diane. Not when a man and woman want each other." His eyes pierced her now with a questioning look. "I can't help but wonder what Mike did to you to make you so afraid of love."

"Afraid?" she echoed, numb with terror at having him get so close to the truth.

He shrugged. "Why else would you want to marry a man you don't love?"

She closed the door on him and leaned her head against it. *Damn him! Damn and double damn him for coming along and messing up her life.*

## - *4* -

DIANE PASSED THE time until six o'clock stewing over how to get out of her date with Greg. She could claim a splitting headache, but he would undoubtedly appear on her doorstep with a bottle of aspirins. Sick children, relatives, and pets were out of the question; she didn't have any. A sudden avalanche of work was implausible; besides, she *wanted* to go to the Saint-Jean. So she gave up, and by six o'clock was dressed and ready when Greg rang the bell.

But when she opened the door, it was as though she had been thinking of another person altogether. The man who stood in her doorway looked boyishly young. His dark, curly hair was still damp from the shower; his white shirt open at the throat showed a muscular brown neck; and the navy wool pullover draped over his shoulders and knotted emphasized the breadth of his chest. The smile he gave her was so frank and warm, the smile of a man about to go out for a good time with his date, that Diane couldn't help but respond. Whatever negative feelings they had about each other were evidently to be put aside on this night of the Saint-Jean.

38

Diane made a last-minute adjustment of her white crocheted top and white skirt. Then they started out for the
other end of the bay, where the festival was taking place.
As they walked along, a banshee wail was borne to them
on the evening breeze.

"Bagpipes?" Greg asked, puzzled.

"It's the Breton bagpipe," Diane explained. "It's called
a *biniou*. I know you got there too late to hear him play
it, but didn't you notice the musical instrument Yann had
at my house this afternoon?"

"I'm afraid my mind was on something else." He gave
her a suggestive look, which she ignored. "Actually," he
went on musingly, "I've seen some pretty strange musical
instruments in my time. A certain African tribe, for ex-
ample, will slit an enormous log to use as a drum, and raise
it on a framework of beams for greater resonance. The
framework is roofed over so the drum will have its own
house. Before it is used, it's sprinkled with blood and prayed
to, and a naming party is held for it. Because many African
languages are tonal, these drums can transmit extremely
intricate messages, and it's amazing to hear them talk to
each other over great distances."

"You didn't happen to record it, did you?" Diane asked
wistfully.

Greg laughed. "It was the last thing on my mind at the
time." More seriously, he added, "I thought singing was
the all-important thing to you."

"It is, but I also collect ethnic music."

"Then I'll send you a record next chance I get," he said
lightly. "What do you fancy? A funeral wailer in Ethiopia?
The chant of a camel driver in Suez?"

"I thought you said this afternoon you would be building
hydroelectric plants in the States."

"But not forever," he said softly. "We could travel all
over the world and make beautiful music together—or at
least record it."

Diane laughed in spite of herself. Then, leery of the
direction the conversation was taking, she started to walk

faster. But he put his arm around her waist and drawled, "Slow down. I've never walked to a Breton folk festival with an opera singer before."

"Whom do you usually take to these affairs?" she asked sweetly. She took his hand and firmly removed it from around her waist, but he wouldn't let go of her hand. There was something innocent, a "first boyfriend" feeling about holding hands, a feeling intensified by the rapid beating of her heart when he interlaced his fingers with hers. They were long and sinewy, and gripped her as though she belonged to him.

"My taste runs to those ancient Celts," he answered loftily. "You know, long red-blond hair, lots of gold—on the arm, not the teeth—and a shoulder-to-toe white bath sheet. Somebody like Norma," he added with an amused sidelong glance at Diane.

"You know opera!" she exclaimed with pleasure.

"Not really. I read up on Bellini last night after I met you."

Diane laughed. "You couldn't have. The Poilvets don't have a book in their house, and they undoubtedly think Bellini is a kind of pasta."

"Don't put down the local gentry! I'll tell Holiday Homes."

Laughing, they threaded their way through the crowd gathered to watch the file of men, women, and children in native costume winding its way down from the headland onto the cement boardwalk bordering the beach. The wail of bagpipes pierced the air and drums kept up a steady accompanying beat.

Diane explained in answer to Greg's questions that the Bretons were descendants of the Celtic people who crossed the Channel from Britain during the Anglo-Saxon invasions of the fifth century. The Breton language, she added, was very similar to Welsh, although not many people spoke either tongue now. And Saint-Cast itself was named for Cado, the son of a sixth-century Irish prince, who became a bishop and after many travels settled in the area.

When the parade was over, the entertainment began.

Children performed folk dances on an elevated platform on the boardwalk. The boys wore short black jackets and hats with broad brims and streamers that hung down their backs. The girls were doll-like in white bonnets, embroidered shawls, and full, bright skirts. A succession of dancers, bands, and singers from the folkloric groups of the area followed. Among them were Yann and his friends, including Guy Kerbellec, who received the most enthusiastic applause of all.

Food stalls had been set up, and women in the tall, white lace caps of old Brittany turned sputtering brown-skinned sausages in long-handled pans or poured batter for that Breton invention—crêpes—onto black iron griddles. Nearby, a scarred wooden table held jugs of homemade apple cider and bottles of whisky. The air was redolent with the pungent, slightly greasy smell of the sizzling, crackling sausages and the sweeter perfume of the pancakes.

Diane and Greg sauntered over to the crêpes stand, where each of them rolled a sausage into a crêpe and ate it like a hot dog. Then they gaily chaffed each other while deciding between lemon or orange crêpes for dessert, or those filled with melted chocolate or cooked with a dash of Grand Marnier or just dripping butter and sugar. Thirsty, they repaired to the drinks table, where men in fishermen's sweaters sat around a flotilla of bottles.

"They look like serious drinkers," Greg said. "Why don't you try the cider, Diane? The whisky's probably rotgut, and there's nothing to mix it with."

"It's more likely Calvados from Normandy—just about the best brandy you can get. But I'll have the cider anyway."

As she had suspected, it was "hard" cider. She didn't particularly want an alcoholic beverage at the moment, but its astringent tartness was welcome after the sweet crêpes she had eaten.

With nightfall, the crowd on the boardwalk flowed over toward the beach. A white line of surf and a rhythmic hiss were the only signs that the blackness out there was ocean. On the beach, men were tying a humanlike figure of straw in a sitting position inside a large wooden rowboat.

"What the hell are they doing?" Greg asked.

"Wait," Diane answered. "You'll see."

A line of men and boys passed a lighted torch from one to the other. The last one touched the straw man with it. Flames shot into the air at the same time that a bonfire on each of the headlands lit the black sky.

"What's it supposed to mean?" Greg said.

"They're celebrating Midsummer Eve, the night of June twenty-third. As I said this afternoon, it's the combination of a summer-solstice festival and the Festival of the Saint-Jean. At one time, every hill in Europe and Britain blazed with a fire on this night. It was the people's way of signaling to each other that summer had finally come, fire representing the sun, of course. But being a seafaring people, these Bretons build their bonfire in a boat."

"And who's the guy in the boat?"

"Nobody really knows; his origins have been lost with the passage of time. My guess is that he's the symbol of winter."

The crowd was now a happy mixture of children and adults eating crêpes and sausages, watching the boat burn, or milling aimlessly about. The whine of bagpipes had given way to the sweet strains of a waltz from the combination casino and dance hall behind the boardwalk. The dance that was part of the Festival of the Saint-Jean had started, and Greg and Diane joined the couples walking toward the hall.

Everyone was dancing—teenagers in blue jeans, their parents, and even *their* parents, and younger brothers and sisters still in Breton costume.

Diane flowed as naturally into Greg's arms as water finding its own level. This was innocent, too, she thought. Men and women danced together all the time. But they didn't dance like this—cheek-to-cheek, heart beating hard to the other heart—if the woman was engaged to be married and the arms about her were those of her future brother-in-law. Of course, the engagement *was* open-ended, and hadn't yet been announced, but still... Yet in the magical atmosphere of the festival, Lyle seemed more removed than ever. Especially when she was enveloped in Greg's masterful arms and giddy with the scent of his spicy aftershave.

Was it true, she wondered, that men who were good dancers were also good lovers? In fantasy, she transferred from the dance floor to the bedroom the sureness with which Greg led her through the intricate steps, his legs moving rhythmically with hers, and the warm smell of his skin. In response to her fantasy, she unconsciously pressed herself a little closer to him.

"You *are* a temptress, Diane," he whispered in a kiss against her cheek. His husky, sexy baritone sent an erotic thrill down her spine, causing it to arch under his hand. He pulled her closer, crushing her breasts against his broad chest.

Dancing like this *was* an act of love, Diane decided. She pulled away and looked for a diversion. Her eyes found Nadia, approaching in the arms of a man Diane didn't know. Nadia's heart-shaped face showed distress, and she was obviously holding herself as far away from her partner's bearlike hug as she could. As they passed, Diane heard the man whisper in a loud, drunken slur, "Lesh go outside." Nadia's violent "No!" was written all over her unhappy face. Why didn't she just break away? Diane wondered, and decided it was probably in fear of making a scene. Nadia had a tendency to be timid, which made her an easy prey for louts like the one she was with now.

Diane lost sight of the pair in the crush of dancers on the floor. Then she picked them up again, leaving the dance hall. Nadia was in the lead, her small mouth set in grim determination, while the fellow, with a drunken leer, stumbled after her. It was not that unfamiliar a scene—a young woman ditching an unwelcome date—but Diane wondered if Nadia could handle the situation. The man had an unmistakably lecherous look on his flushed face, and Nadia was so tiny.

Where was Guy? He would make mincemeat of anyone who bothered his sister. Diane scanned the room, but couldn't find him. Greg would help, but she felt reluctant to drag him into the affair. Besides, all it would take was one person—any person—to give Nadia the protection she might need.

The song ended. Diane let Greg escort her off the floor, then she excused herself to go to the ladies' room. Instead, she went out into the dark night, where the only light came from the windows of the casino and the only sound at first seemed to be the dance music. But Diane soon heard the sighs and whispers and small groans of lovers coming from the pines behind the building. She stood still for a moment, listening for Nadia's voice. Then she heard it, a mixture of fear and defiance and protest, as she evidently tried to fight off her attacker.

Diane ran in the direction of the girl's voice and reached her just in time to see two figures struggling in the dark. But both were too burly to be Nadia. Diane saw one of the men fall to the ground, and surmised that Guy had finally come to the rescue of his little sister. She waited until, her eyes more accustomed to the dark, she saw Guy put his arm around Nadia's shoulder and lead her away. Then Diane left the grove, a smile quirking the corners of her lips. Who was Guy's girlfriend? She didn't know he had a romantic interest. Her smile deepened as she reflected that he was probably leaving a very diappointed woman among the pine trees.

She glanced toward the dance hall. Greg would be wondering where she was. She took a step toward the building, then stopped. Greg would think it shabby of her, but it might be better if she didn't return. The seductive way he slid his hand up and down her spine, the feel of him as he pressed his hard length against her, even the symbolism implicit in their bodies moving together in perfect harmony, all spelled temptation. She thought she was strong enough not to yield to it, but why invite trouble?

Diane walked past the dance hall to the boardwalk. It was deserted now. She looked out toward the beach. The boat was still burning—its wooden skeleton outlined in the darkness by the orange flames. On impulse, she walked down the stairs for a closer look.

She stood and stared for a long time into the dancing flames. According to an old Breton belief, a young girl who wanted to be married in the coming year had to visit nine of these midsummer bonfires.

But *she* didn't have to visit nine fires. She was to be married in the coming year. And if her husband-to-be didn't light any fires in her, that wasn't so important, was it? She could hardly be a pawn to passion and a self-disciplined artist at the same time.

A hand on her shoulder turned her slowly. She knew whose it was. A case in point, she thought wryly. Greg's touch might fire her like a spark on straw, but it was only a physical thing, nothing to take really seriously.

"That's not very nice, to run out on a guy, especially the waltz king of Brittany."

Diane laughed nervously. "I felt a little dizzy from the hard cider and the heat in the room. I thought I'd recover faster if I got some fresh air." Coward! she thought. But what else could she have said? If she revealed how much he attracted her, that would encourage him even more.

"You owe me something for walking out on me," he insisted.

"Not a dance!" she said, laughing again. "Not on this sand."

"No, this." Still holding her, he brought his mouth down to hers with a hot, firm sweetness that seemed to course through her body, leaving her languid and ready in his arms. And when he finally let her go, she waited, lips parted, the tension in her spiraling painfully upward until his mouth fastened on hers again. But this time he played with her. His lips barely brushed hers. His teeth bit gently at her full lower lip. His tongue licked sensually at the corners. Avid for more, she pushed her mouth restlessly against his, dissatisfied with the desire this man had aroused within her, impatient to have it assuaged and done with. At the same time, she wrapped her arms around him, moving her fingers

lightly across his broad back, reveling in the feel of his lean
flesh and strong muscles. Instantly, the length of him went
hard and male. His arms swept her in so close to him, they
seemed fused into one being, one mouth, giving and demanding, with neither knowing which.

When she broke away, she was shaking. Head bent to
his chest, she murmured, "I'm afraid I'm still feeling the
effects of that cider. Or maybe it's the new moon." Forcing
a laugh, she pointed to the thin crescent in the black sky.
"At any rate, let's not do that again, okay, Greg?"

He didn't answer, and she took a step past him toward
the boardwalk.

"I'll see you home."

"No," she said shortly, "I'd rather you didn't."

The steady hiss and roar of the ocean went on behind
her. The boat still burned brightly on the sand. The flames
lit Greg's watchful face; he had the quiet look of a man
preparing to take what he wanted.

Then, as she moved into the darkness, he caught up with
her. Before she could flee or protest, his large hands closed
around her slim sides. Heart pounding, she slowly turned
and his mouth came down again on her softly parted lips.

"Diana, moon goddess," he whispered. "My temptress."
And he cupped her breasts until she felt them apple-heavy
in his hands.

His hand reached inside her crocheted top. Slowly, he
slid it off one shoulder. Then, leaning over her, he painted
her smooth skin with kisses.

When he bared the other shoulder, he let his hand linger
on its satiny surface before sliding it down over the first
upward swell of her breast. As his fingers splayed across
the soft flesh, the nipple peaking under them, he bent his
head and took her lips again. After a long, tender kiss, he
stroked her lips with his firm, sure tongue, then thrust it
gently into the warm recesses of her mouth.

Her whole body was throbbing with desire now. *This is
madness*, she told herself. *Midsummer madness*.

"No!" she half-whispered, half-shouted, pushing him violently away. *"No!* Leave me alone or I'll . . . I'll tell Lyle."

He threw his head back and laughed. She stared at him, rooted to the spot as she had been the first time she saw him.

There was so much pagan joy in his wide-legged stance, the tight chinos he had on like his own tanned flesh, and so much freedom in his laugh that when he placed one hand lightly on her hip, she became like a woman bewitched. She stood like that, letting his lips rove across her soft flesh for the places they wanted to kiss until they trapped the pulse in her throat as it beat a strong "Yes! Yes!"

She shivered, but not from cold.

"I'll warm you," he said huskily. He smoothed his hands along her shoulders until she thought she could feel their touch in her very bones. He slid her loose-weave top all the way to her waist. The warmth of his large hands as they moved over her shoulders and sides and lace-cupped breasts seemed to fire her blood. The dark night and pagan ritual, his fire-bronzed face and elemental maleness, all affected her strangely. She felt primitive and defenseless against herself.

Afraid of what was happening inside her, she pulled her top up, then turned silently and ran across the sand. When she reached the concrete walk, she looked down at the beach. She knew he was still there, standing in the dark.

Looking far-eyed out into the distance, she saw a surreal image of herself poised there on the boardwalk as though in front of a three-way mirror—Mike's nice little wife, Lyle's society queen, and Greg's . . . what?

Later that night, under the sloping ceiling of her aunt's second-story bedroom, Diane looked out at the hilltop bonfire still burning. Someone must have thrown more wood on, because the flames seemed to be leaping up toward the tender, young moon.

The moon on fire, she mused, intrigued by the idea.

Moon goddess on fire, she added ruefully, recalling her reaction to Greg's kisses.

Then she laughed out loud, a low, musical ripple of amusement at herself. Watch it, moon goddess, she warned herself, you'll be saying "You Tarzan, Me Jane" next.

She narrowed her eyes in the darkness. Midsummer's Eve was notorious for causing sensible people to do foolish things. But the night of the Saint-Jean was over. From now on, any relationship with her future brother-in-law would be strictly business or family.

# - 5 -

FOR A WHOLE week after the Saint-Jean, Diane threw herself into her singing with impassioned self-discipline. Opening the window wide early each morning, she performed breathing and relaxation exercises to assure an even flow of breath and good tone production. Starting her vocal practice, she did elaborate exercises with vowels to make her voice bigger and a clear, even exaggerated, pronunciation of vowels automatic. Then came vocalization, a seemingly endless singing of scales and repeated mouthings of A, E, I, O, U.

Using a mirror to watch her mouth and jaw movements, she worked on her *legato,* the smooth linking of musical notes without any sliding from one to the other. If she didn't hit each note squarely, her vocal coach in Rennes, Madame Daudon, would make her do the exercise over and over, ten or fifteen times—as often as it took to get it right—and then another ten times to make the right way automatic.

Diane didn't like Madame Daudon, and she was afraid the lack of rapport between them was affecting her singing. It was not because the teacher was a hard taskmaster; Diane approved of perfectionism as the only way to excellence.

But why did Madame Daudon give herself such ridiculous airs? She looked down on everything Breton and referred to herself always as Parisian, even though she had lived in Rennes with her husband for at least ten years. More important, she never let Diane forget that she had sung with the Paris Opera, whereas, she implied, it was doubtful that Diane, even with the expert teaching she was finally receiving, would ever fulfill her dreams of singing grand opera.

Diane had a hard time evaluating Madame Daudon's criticism of her voice and technique. She knew she had problem areas. She still had trouble occasionally with her *passaggio*, the movement of the voice from one register to another, but her Chicago teacher thought that the changing of gears, as singers called it, would not be noticeable to an audience. Madame Daudon, however, had the unnerving habit of crashing her hands down on the piano keys like thunder when Diane didn't bring off this technique.

Still, Monique Daudon had been recommended to Diane as the best vocal coach in the area, so every afternoon Diane faithfully drove her aunt's old car to Rennes for two hours of exacting work. Naturally, Madame Daudon was well versed in the repertoire of French opera, as was Diane. Together, they selected an aria from *Esclarmonde* for Diane's audition song. Diane got a secret kick out of the fact that the composer, Jules Massenet, had written the opera for a soprano from Sacramento named Sibyl Sanderson, who went to Paris and became the belle of La Belle Epoque—and, it was said, the mistress of the great man himself.

For fear of meeting Greg, Diane even denied herself the beach during this time. In lieu of her morning run, she jumped rope and did calisthenics. But nothing could replace the wonderful high she got from running. She began to feel sluggish and out of sorts. Then one morning she had to tug at the zipper on her jeans to close it. She looked down in disbelief and saw a slight but unmistakable bellying out of soft flesh. That night she set her alarm for six o'clock and put out her navy-blue jogging suit and white scarf.

It was still dark when a nervous, insistent jangling clanged through the room. Diane reached out a hand to the old-fashioned Baby Ben and pressed the alarm button down. But the ringing continued, and Diane reluctantly got out of bed and padded barefoot to the telephone. Vanessa's flat midwestern tones twanged over the wires, first strong, then faint, then strong again, so that Diane had a mental picture of that imperious voice commanding the elements of air and water to be still while it spoke.

"Diane, did I take you away from something? This is Vanessa."

"Only bed." Diane glanced at the illuminated clock dial. "It's four A.M. here."

"Is it! I never can remember when your people begin observing daylight-saving time."

Diane started a slow burn as she always did when Vanessa hinted that she was more French than American. *"My* people have been on daylight-saving time from New York to California since the middle of April, Vanessa."

"Well, the reason I called is to let you know that I'll be arriving in Brittany sometime tomorrow. I'm flying from Chicago to London and from there to Dinard."

Diane mustered up a weak "Wonderful!" from reserves of hypocrisy she didn't know she had. But for Lyle's sake, she had decided to let bygones be bygones. "Why don't you plan on staying with me, Vanessa? There's plenty of room in my aunt's house."

"Thank you, Diane," Vanessa said coolly, "but I've already made a reservation at the Grand Hotel in Dinard."

"May I pick you up at the Dinard airport, then? It's only fifteen miles from Saint-Cast."

"That won't be necessary, either. The hotel has an airport service."

So much for burying the hatchet, Diane thought, as she uttered a noncommittal "Oh."

After a long silence during which Diane wondered if her future sister-in-law's voice hadn't drowned for good, Vanessa said in a resigned tone, "Lyle will be here in a few days, as soon as he brings certain financial arrangements to a close." Vanessa was always closemouthed about the family-owned business, and was obviously reluctant to see the engaged couple come together.

"That's marvelous," Diane said impulsively. "Greg's here, so it'll be a family get-together." She was disciplining herself to think of Greg in that way, as a member of the family she would soon be part of instead of a man to whom she was strongly attracted. If the fostering of certain images helped people stop smoking, why wouldn't it help with other addictions?

"Of course we'll want to see you and Greg," Vanessa answered with evasive, sugary cordiality. Then, with a promise to call Diane after she had rested from the long flight, she hung up.

Diane went back to bed, but not to sleep. Vanessa's snobbishness was ridiculous. Naturally, she'd rather tell her cronies in Forestville that she had stayed at the best hotel in a prestigious little seaside resort frequented only by those "in the know" than in an ordinary house in middle-class Saint-Cast. But Vanessa was also strong-willed and no fool. And although Lyle was the most democratic of men, he was basically as conventional as his sister. Between the two of them, it was just possible they would succeed in molding her into what they wanted—a Kimball wife, beautiful, well dressed, and socially accomplished. Vanessa would conceive of this transformation as Diane's duty; Lyle would see it as an act of love, as giving her everything a woman could possibly want. With a shiver of fear, Diane even saw herself somehow being finessed out of an operatic career.

Her muscles tensed. Her body was preparing itself to fight or flee, but not to sleep. Vanessa, like Macbeth, had murdered sleep. Diane sprang out of bed and, pulling up the blind, was surprised to see the sun was up, bright and warm. With a whoop of joy, she scrambled out of her pajamas, then stood irresolute in the middle of the bedroom floor. It might even, at last, be warm enough for swimming.

Washing quickly, she pulled on a blue and turquoise mitered-stripe maillot—a swimmer's suit with sensible straps—and threw a gauzy white cover-up over it.

She ran through the stand of pines, across the boardwalk, and over the empty sands to the water's edge. It seemed to her that the sea lay flat like a harp, the waves burning like wires under the golden sun. *Arcoat*—the wood. *Armor*—the sea. Ocean and forest—the whole of Brittany was illustrated by these two ancient words. For Diane, the sea was always paramount. She stood on her toes and held her face out to its sharp, tangy smell, letting the breeze off the Channel plaster the sheer beach coat to her full breasts and supple form. Standing there, drinking in the crystalline air, she felt all the tension of the morning phone call drain out of her, leaving her buoyant and fresh and happy.

She became conscious then of someone to the side of her. She turned and her eyes met the intensely admiring gaze of Greg Kimball.

"You looked like a figurehead just then," he said. "Like the carved wooden form of a woman on the bow of an old sailing ship."

Surprised like that, with no time to prepare herself for meeting him, she felt her heart begin to beat rapidly and she bit her lower lip in annoyance. It didn't help that, dressed for swimming, he was nearly as devastatingly godlike as he had been the first time she saw him on that beach. The snow-white swim trunks pasted on his small hips and tanned skin appeared merely postage-stamp size on that big frame.

"I'm glad you have something on this time," she said tartly.

"Are you, Diane?" His eyes laughed openly at her, at the same time that his husky baritone caressed her, sending shivers up her spine.

To change the subject, Diane said, "Vanessa called in the wee hours of the morning."

"Vanessa *would*." He waited, his eyes never leaving her face.

"She's arriving tomorrow. Lyle will be here, too, in a few days. We're to have a family get-together then." Diane emphasized *family*.

"I can't believe Vanessa said that." He grinned at her. "Outcasts, that's us." He waved his arm widely at the bay and a white platform bobbing gently in its calm water. "Marooned on a desert island. Can you swim?" He eyed the form-fitting maillot under the transparent cover-up.

"Of course! I grew up here, don't forget."

"I'll race you to the float."

"Easy!" Diane boasted. Stripping off her wrap, she ran beside him into the water. The shock of its coldness took her breath for a moment, then she neatly cleaved the surface and, using her powerful crawl, cut twin furrows with him through the green water. He got to the float before her. Out of practice, she had to rest a short distance away. Instantly, he was beside her.

"Are you all right?" he asked in a voice resonant with concern.

She smiled affirmatively.

He paced her to the float then and, hoisting himself on top of it in one easy motion, reached down to pull her up. His strong hands on the wet suit, which clung to her like a second skin, sent a dangerous thrill radiating through her. She pushed his hands away and stretched out on the platform, giving herself over to its gentle rocking motion and the warmth of the sun.

"You look relaxed enough to go to sleep," Greg said, smiling down at her. "It's like being on a water bed, isn't it? The biggest water bed in the world."

*Bed* wasn't a subject Diane wanted to explore with Greg. "You beat me, fair and square," she said. "You're a strong swimmer."

"If it hadn't been for you, I'd be on my way to England now," he answered lightly. He lowered himself down beside her, and she was acutely aware of his muscular brown legs and the virile dark hair that covered them. His hips nudged hers, causing an instantaneous explosion of heat within her.

She moved restlessly, and he propped himself up on one elbow and glanced at her. Then his caressing gaze journeyed the terrain of her body, molded by the maillot into glorious curves and valleys. Bending his head, he whispered to her and to the clear air and a seagull flying by, "You smell sun-warmed and sweet and salty, all at the same time."

She sat up. "I'm ready to swim back now."

"You can't yet. I haven't collected."

"Collected what?"

"Whatever I won in that swimming race."

"Let's make it two out of three," Diane said with a laugh, rising to her feet. "Come on, I'll race you back."

But as she poised herself to dive, she felt his hands on her hips, pulling her back.

"Sharks!" he whispered dramatically in her ear.

She turned in the encircling arms and, laughing, gave him a little push. "The only shark is right here!"

"And sharks eat little fish." So saying, he held her close and nibbled seductively at her ear and neck. As his hands slid down her bare back, her body began to tremble. His chest was a wall that stopped her thrusting breasts; the way his manly brown fur feathered the soft flesh that rose from the top of her swimsuit was deliciously exciting. His warm thighs pressed against hers, and as they clung to each other like shipwrecked survivors, she could feel his arousal hard against her complementing softness. With a sharp intake of breath, she turned her face up to the honeyed lips that had beguiled her with their wizardry on the night of the Festival of the Saint-Jean.

Only then did she remember where they were. Smiling impishly, she murmured, "We're in full view of the beach, Greg."

His mouth half covering hers in a greedy kiss, he whispered huskily, "Let's teach the French how to make love."

For an answer, she laughed her low musical laugh and pushed him away. Then she dove off the side of the float and made for shore.

This time, she beat him in the race and stood waiting

for him to come striding toward her out of the surf. "We're even now," he called out. "How about tomorrow?"

She shook her head in a laughing no and, picking up her wrap, started to walk briskly along the beach.

He caught up with her and said, "What's the rush?"

"I'm too tired after that little workout to jog, so I'm going to walk for a while."

"Hey, lady, you don't want to walk alone; this beach is full of muggers."

She glanced around at the solitary French family crossing the sand in single file and, matching his tone, said, "Sure, buster."

They walked along side by side in silence for a while, stopping at times to watch a pelican skim the water on its morning fishing run or a seagull staring out to sea like a Nantucket whaling widow, soberly dressed in white and gray.

"Poor birds!" Diane said with a laugh. "We were such naughty children! Yann and Guy and I used to ride our bikes to a place several miles from here and climb the cliffs to rob the gannets' nests of their eggs—actually one egg, because that's all they produce at a time. It was very dangerous—the cliffs rise right out of the sea—and of course it was wrong from an ecological point of view. But it was a game, to see who could get the most eggs."

"Did you come to Saint-Cast often with your parents?" he asked.

"Sometimes I came alone and stayed with my aunt. Sometimes my mother came, too. Never my father; even before their divorce." She laughed shortly. "Life in a little one-horse French town wasn't exciting enough for him."

He looked at her inquiringly, and Diane quickly turned the conversation to general subjects—opera, French wines, his work. She found him well-informed but not pedantic; sophisticated in his tastes but not blasé. His reasoning was careful and thorough, as befitted an engineer. This was no fly-by-night adventurer, but a man of solid accomplishments. She liked him, she decided. Once she was married to Lyle, the physical attraction between them would certainly vanish, and then she and Greg could be friends. She made a little face as she strode along beside him. Lyle had some old-fashioned ideas. One was that they shouldn't sleep together until their wedding night. It was almost two years since Mike had passed away, and he had been ill for a year before that. No wonder, she thought, she was so responsive to this attentive, virile man beside her.

As they returned to the boardwalk, Greg asked, "How about coffee at my place? I'll stand treat for the croissants and *Herald Tribune* this time."

"Thanks, but I won't have time. I'm going to have to start practicing the minute I get home."

"Would you consider a trip to the Rance hydroelectric plant this afternoon?"

Diane laughed. That Rance plant again! "I have a lesson with my vocal coach in Rennes every afternoon."

"I'll buy you lunch first."

"Not before I sing!" Diane said, shocked. "A heavy meal would interfere with my breathing."

"A couple of oysters won't hurt you," he answered stoutly. She hesitated. His remark about her having always to plan ahead and control events still rankled. She wondered briefly if the rigid schedule that she had, of necessity, imposed on herself hadn't robbed her of spontaneity. Perhaps she should do the unexpected for a change. Something in her expression must have given her vacillation away, for Greg said, "Then it's settled. I'll pick you up at twelve, regale you with bivalves, and take you to your lesson."

# - 6 -

WHEN SHE GOT HOME, the delicious feeling she had of flirting with danger played havoc with her scales and arpeggios. Ordinarily very conscientious, this time she didn't care. Her mind kept veering off from the notes she was singing to what she would wear to lunch. And instead of watching her mouth in the mirror for its enunciation, she found herself checking its kissable qualities.

Feeling daring, she dressed accordingly in a back-buttoned, plunging-V mini of black cotton with white pin dots. Madame Daudon would undoubtedly be shocked, but so what? Minis were all the rage in France that year, and Diane had the legs for them.

She picked the restaurant, a place in the fishing port of Cancale famous for its oysters. Tables had been set up outside, and Greg chose one with a view of the fishing boats and nets spread out on the quay to dry. At his suggestion, Diane ordered for them both. She chose the prized Belon oysters, served in cracked ice on the top tier of a metal trestle; on the tier below were thin slices of buttered brown bread, a dish of shallots, and a bowl of vinegar.

After the first one, Greg said in amazement, "I've never had oysters like these. You can still taste the sea in them."

Diane giggled. "French oysters are trained to close their valves so as to retain the sea water in their shells."

"You're kidding!" he said with marked disbelief.

"No, it's true. There's a whole thing about the cultivation of oysters," she added with a dismissive wave of her hand.

She had planned on having only oysters and mineral water so as to be in condition for the strenuous singing ahead of her, but Greg persuaded her to have a glass of the dry, fruity white wine of Brittany called Muscadet because of its slight flavor of nutmeg, *muscade* in French. After the oysters, Greg complained of still being hungry, so she ordered a *cotriade,* a fish chowder that was a cousin of the more famous *bouillabaisse* of Marseilles, for him and, so he wouldn't have to eat alone, one for herself. That required more wine, and what with the sun and the sparkle of the day and the vibrant eyes of the man across from her, lingering with flattering pleasure on her face and bare, rounded arms, Diane felt just a little woozy when she got up from the white wrought-iron chair.

Greg's strong arm supported her, and his eyes, golden-brown now in the sun, gleamed with amusement as he deposited her in his car.

"Sure you don't want to play hookey?" he asked with a sidelong glance at her.

"I can't! Madame Daudon would strangle me with her own arthritic hands. Not that I'm in any shape for a lesson. You shouldn't have lured me into that huge lunch," she wailed.

"It was all I *could* lure you into."

She gave a little grunt and rolled down the window. Fresh air was what she needed. But the wine made her drowsy before the air could revive her, and she ended up drifting off into sleep against Greg's shoulder. She woke up once, saw that he was driving with one hand, and murmured, "That's against the law." Subliminally, she knew that his other arm was around her, but it felt so good to be held close to him and she felt too weary to protest. So when he gave her a squeeze and said, *"This* is against the law? I don't believe it; not in France," she didn't correct him.

Two hours later, give or take a few minutes, she was back in his car, this time parked on a narrow street in Rennes.

"How did you like the Breton folk museum?" she asked, since that was where Greg had said he would spend his waiting time.

He rolled his eyes comically. "I think that's where the Poilvets bought their furniture. How'd your lesson go?"

"I have no idea; the whole thing was a blur. I'm sure the only reason Madame Daudon didn't throw me out is she was afraid she wouldn't be paid."

An engaging grin lit his strong features. He reached out his arm for her.

Edging away, she sang out, "But I'm sober now. *Cold* sober."

He threw the car in gear and adroitly steered it between a double phalanx of parked cars. "Just so long as you're not sober *and cold,*" he said with a slyly amused look.

"Nice of you to look out for your brother's interest," she riposted.

"I *am* looking out for my brother's interest," he replied. Reminded of his remark about her engagement being unfair to Lyle as well as to herself, Diane stared out the window in a now-familiar feeling of troubled uncertainty.

When they were a few miles from Saint-Cast, she pointed seaward at the cliffs and said, "That's where we used to hunt birds' eggs."

"Want to try it again?"

Diane laughed. "I think I've outgrown robbing nests." She added wistfully, "There's a terrific view from those cliffs, though, and it's interesting to see the baby gannets. They're hatched naked and blind, you know. Then they grow white down, and after that brown feathers speckled with white."

"No, I didn't know," Greg said dryly. He pulled the car

way over to the side of the road and stopped the motor. "Why don't you show me?"

"It's a tough climb up to where the nests are," Diane warned.

He took her hand and placed it on his thigh. "Feel those climbing muscles."

Diane snatched her hand away and said with mock hauteur, "I don't think I care to, thanks." Even in that brief moment, the feel of his hard sinews under her hand had sent a tremor of excitement through her.

"Well, are we going or aren't we?"

"I'm afraid we're not, Greg. The damp sea air would be bad for my throat."

Silently, he reached into the backseat and fetched a heavy white pullover. He draped it over her shoulders and tied the arms around her neck, letting his hands linger. Diane felt that she would like to lean into his hands, to be a cat and have him stroke her. She looked through the car window at the sky. The sun was still bright, and for once there wasn't a single Breton cloud visible. She fingered the thick wool around her neck. Why not go? she thought. This was her "day off," the first in a long time. What harm would an hour on the cliffs do? She wasn't dressed for climbing, but the short dress would give her legs plenty of freedom once she had shed her pantyhose.

"Turn your head, please," she said. "If we're going climbing, I'll have to take my stockings off."

"This is the hardest thing I've ever done," he said, but he obediently turned his back to her.

Then they were out of the car and setting off briskly for the gorse-covered outcropping of rock that loomed ahead of them.

Holding on to boulders and strongly rooted shrubs, with Greg going first and reaching out a hand to Diane, they gradually made their way up the steep cliff. As they went, the broad sea that lay beneath them and the black rocks at the cliff's base, ruffed with the white spume of crashing waves, became ever smaller.

Then Diane whispered "There!" and pointed to a nest of seaweed and grasses out on a ledge. Lifting her eyes, she saw the white and brown plumage, long beaks, and yellow necks of large numbers of birds. The rock seemed alive with them as they waddled around on it; took off to skim the water and, with folded wings, dove for fish; or alighted from a sky that, Diane was horrified to see, was no longer a cloudless blue.

Involuntarily, she breathed, "Oh, God!"

"What is it?" Greg's voice was sharp with concern.

"The fog! Look at it. We'll never get off these cliffs now."

Opaquely white, the fog steamrolled everything—the sea, the birds, and the rocky ledge—out of sight with amazing rapidity. Its acrid smell was sharp in their nostrils, and its dampness clutched at their throats. It muffled the angry churning of the sea beneath them and the lonely mewing of gulls. Diane put her hand on Greg's arm to feel the solid reality of it. Quickly, he encircled her waist. "It's like standing at the edge of the world," he said in an awed voice.

"It's my fault." Her voice was bitter with self-reproach. "I'm the native—or almost. I should have remembered. The fog can roll in from the sea in just a few minutes, especially this late in the afternoon."

"But it was sunny," he remonstrated.

"That doesn't matter." She looked around at the small area of visibility left to them. "We'd better find a hole in the ground and crawl into it. And there goes my operatic career," she added bitterly. "There's nothing like a foggy night by the sea for a singer's vocal cords." She was furious with herself for having dimmed her dream of success by an impulsive act. She didn't even understand how she could have behaved with such uncharacteristic insouciance.

"We'll just have to do the best we can." Greg untied the sweater from around her neck, retied it around his waist, and put the end of it in her hands. "Hang on to that. We're going to explore as far as we can see. There may be a little cave or an opening in the rock that'll shelter us for the night."

Carefully, they groped their way along until Greg called out, "Here's something." He guided Diane's hand horizontally along a flat stone slab, then down the sides of two large vertical stones that supported it like a table.

"It's a dolmen," Diane said. "Brittany is full of them. The prehistoric people who lived here and in Britain built them as burying chambers." Her mood lightened. "That was a lucky find, Greg. It's not the Ritz, but it's a damn sight better than being out in the open all night."

"Let me go first." He crawled into the narrow opening, then stretched out his hand to her. She made her way on her hands and knees until she reached space in the soft, dry gorse that was big enough to lie down on. Greg lay down beside her and put his arm around her shoulder, cradling her against him.

She tensed up, troubled by his closeness and by her thoughts. How could she have been so reckless as to go cliff climbing in the late afternoon when fog could almost be expected? The damage to her throat might be permanent. Even that heavy lunch was stupid. She had wasted two hours of valuable instruction, and Madame Daudon's lessons weren't inexpensive.

What had come over her? Did she want to be with Greg so badly that she would put opera in second place? She had practiced carelessly after their morning swim, had accepted his luncheon invitation against her better judgment, and had actually suggested that they come up on the cliffs to look for birds' nests!

Was this joy in laughing with him, this longing for his kisses, this letting slip away everything for which she had worked so hard, symptomatic of simple physical attraction, intensified by years of denial? Or was it something worse? Was she—and let the answer be no, she silently prayed—falling in love with Greg Kimball?

Panic seized her at this possibility. She couldn't let it

happen—couldn't endanger her career and break her commitment, albeit nonbinding, to Lyle. She pushed forcefully at Greg and rolled away from him. But she came up immediately against solid rock, one of the walls of the dolmen. There was no place to go. She had no choice but to ruin her singer's throat forever in the fog outside or spend the night in the arms of the man it was dangerous for her to be near.

"What's wrong?" Greg asked.

"Nothing. Just a touch of claustrophobia." Not for the world would she let him know how she felt. And she hadn't lied. Her disturbing thoughts *had* made her feel a little suffocated.

"No need to push the panic button," he said with hearty reassurance. "I'll use the emergency phone, and the maintenance men will get us out of here in no time. Besides, there's no place like a stalled elevator for making new friends."

In spite of herself, Diane laughed. "Sounds as though there'd be too many ups and downs in those friendships."

"But for a while, at least, one couldn't kiss and run."

He reached out for her then, but she pushed his arm away. She felt trembly and frightened as a young deer. The little cave seemed to reverberate with an antiphony of voices: one chorus urged her to go to him; the other scolded and shrieked warnings.

"Diane, don't push me away. I'm not going to do anything you don't want me to. But it's going to be a cold, damp night, and if we don't keep each other warm, we'll both end up sick. Think of your throat."

What he had said was true, of course. At all costs, she must protect herself from catching a cold; so she drew close to him again and fitted her body against his. The feel of his muscles and flesh against her side and hip and leg was torture to Diane. It aroused wild longings in her for the adventure of his touch and the searing pressure of his lips against hers. She could hear the steady thump of his heart, and his quickened breath fanned her cheek. Remembering the ardor of his embraces the night of the Saint-Jean, she thought, this must be difficult for him, too. A slight flirtation was one thing, but this semi-cave was the setting for a more primal relationship.

"Talking helps if you really feel claustrophobic." He began to stroke her hair gently, and slowly she felt herself relax under his caress. "You're pretty young to have lost a husband. How did you feel when Mike died? Were you all broken up?"

"No. I was exhausted from taking care of him and very sad, but I wasn't devastated. The truth is, I had stopped loving him some time before. In fact, I was planning a divorce when Mike told me he had cancer. I wouldn't leave him after that, and I stayed with him until the end."

"What happened to make you stop loving him?"

Perhaps because it was dark, so that she couldn't see his face and he couldn't see hers, or perhaps because his voice was tender and caring, Diane felt an urge to tell Greg what she had kept hidden from everyone, even Lyle.

"Mike was the proverbial traveling salesman," she said ruefully. *"That's* when I was all broken up—when I found out the first time. I was crazy about him; but then when he continued having affairs, I gradually stopped loving him. I didn't want to live with a man like that. I didn't want children by him."

"Then you're marrying steady, reliable Lyle because he's so different from Mike."

The vehemence of her answer surprised even her. "No! All men are the same. Mike taught me that. Only, married to Lyle, it won't hurt so much."

Greg was silent for a moment. "I would hazard a guess," he said slowly, "that Mike told you men have different sexual requirements than women; that they need various partners. It's in their genes."

"That's right," she said defiantly. "Can you deny it?"

"I've known plenty of women bed-hoppers in my time."

"Well, I'm not a bed-hopper, and neither was my mother."

As soon as the words left her mouth, Diane regretted

them. She had never told anyone but Mike about her father's frequent absences and her mother's shrill accusations, uttered when Mrs. James thought their little girl was asleep. Diane had only once confided in Mike, when she herself lost control and quarreled bitterly with him over one of his sexual escapades. His response had been a bland "That's the only reason you're upset—because your mother over-reacted with your dad. If she had been more reasonable, you would be, too."

"There are no guarantees in life," Greg said thoughtfully. "You've got to give to get, and if you're too afraid to give, you end up with a relationship like the one you have with Lyle."

"How often do I have to tell you that there's nothing wrong with my relationship with Lyle?" she screamed at him.

"Don't be a fool, Diane." The words were breathed softly on her face as he leaned over her in the darkness and trailed his fingers along her jaw. She doubled her hands into fists and raised them to his chest. She would not endure another assault on her senses. She would fight him off before she would let him kiss her again.

But as she drew one tightly clenched fist back for a blow, his mouth came down softly over her own. At the gentle touch of his lips, an ineffable sweetness, a honey-slow languor, invaded her body. Her hands opened until her palms rested lightly on his chest. The kiss deepened with a throbbing, insistent entreaty as his mouth played demandingly against hers. Now her hands crept around his neck and nestled inside his shirt, against his warm flesh. The questing tip of his tongue nudged enticingly at her lips, outlining their shape, and now and again touching aggressively at a corner. Under the persistent thrusts, her lips softly parted and his tongue engaged hers in a love duet that sent delicious tremors of excitement through her.

Diane was in a delirium of joy, all her senses ablaze with desire. His hands were around her now, gliding across the thick pullover she had donned and then up under it to the thin cotton dress. She had so yearned to feel his hands on her and her nerves were tuned to such a high pitch by the day's events, that a long shudder racked her body. His strong frame trembled against hers in response. With one hand splayed across her back and the other under her thighs, he raised her to him. He kissed her fiercely, forcing her lips apart almost brutally so that his strong teeth grazed hers.

Then, slowly, he withdrew his mouth from hers and lowered her to the ground.

"I won't take what's Lyle's," he said bitterly.

There was nothing she could say to that. Nothing. She couldn't even think about what was happening to her. A fog as thick as the one on the cliffs seemed suddenly to have formed the climate of her mind. All she could do was lie beside him, the two of them rigid with unsatisfied desire, silent and careful not to touch.

Finally, his voice rough, Greg said, "What are your chances of passing the audition, do you think?"

Diane was grateful to him for launching an innocuous subject of conversation. "I don't want to sound overconfident, but I think they're good. I won a singing scholarship in college, I've sung in a number of operettas, and my voice teachers have said they thought I have what it takes." All except Madame Daudon, she reflected wryly.

"Well, save me two tickets, goddess. I'll come to hear you sing."

"Two tickets?"

"Sure, for me and a lady friend. You don't think I'd go to the opera by myself, do you?"

"I hadn't thought about it at all," she said coolly. But she knew the edge in her voice was a carry-over from the ridiculous stab of jealousy she had felt when he mentioned a "lady friend." And judging from his chuckle there in the dark, he knew it, too. With an exasperated grunt, she turned away from him and gradually drifted off to sleep.

The next morning, although tattered rags of fog still clung to the cliffs, it was clear enough for Greg and Diane to start climbing down. When they reached the car, they drove to Saint-Cast, past dew-covered fields and ghostly oaks shrouded with mistletoe.

"I could sure use a cup of coffee," Greg said as they entered the town. "Your place or mine?"

"It's my turn."

"True, but I offered first. Remember that croissant party I invited you to yesterday morning?"

"It seems like ages ago," she mused.

"You're right, so let's eat them before they're hard as that dolmen we slept under last night."

A short while later, he was pulling up in front of the Poilvet house and opening the front door.

"I should have gone home," Diane said, glancing down at herself. "Strange as it may seem, I look as though I slept in my clothes; and worse, I think I'm getting a sore throat."

This had been her secret worry all along, that she would get sick. She had been trying the power of positive thinking, willing her body to resist the consequences of a night spent in the open. It had seemed to work until just a few minutes ago, when her throat began to feel raspy and raw.

As she stood, irresolute, in the foyer, he said, "A hot shower and hot coffee are what you need. Go take your shower while I make the coffee. There's a robe hanging on a hook in the bathroom. You can wrap yourself in that when you're finished."

The warm needles of water drove all the aches and pains of the night from her body, the steam seemed to soothe her sore throat, and Greg's terry-cloth robe enveloped her like a white bearskin. Barefoot and with a towel turbaning her gleaming hair, she was on her way to the kitchen, when the doorbell rang.

"I'll get it!" she called out. She opened the door and looked straight into the aristocratic features of Vanessa Kimball. Diane watched as Vanessa's pale blue eyes went wide with amazement, then half closed in a calculating, triumphant gleam.

# - 7 -

A TREMOR OF fear ran through Diane. No matter how much she resisted it, face to face Vanessa always had a terrifying effect on her. The combination of the older woman's smooth poise and barely concealed disdain brought out latent feelings of social inferiority that Diane despised but couldn't help. And it was obvious that nothing could have suited Vanessa more than to catch the "temptress" in a state of undress with Lyle's illegitimate half-brother.

Glancing up, Diane saw that Greg had joined her at the door; judging from the twitching of his lips and the gleam in his eyes, it was all he could do to keep from laughing. Giving her a conspiratorial glance, he planted himself firmly at her side. A warm rush of friendship and camaraderie swept Diane. Feeling more confident with this stalwart ally beside her, she opened the door wider and said courteously, "How nice to see you, Vanessa."

Greg's deep voice echoed her sentiments. "Come in, Vanessa. Diane and I are recovering from an adventure on the cliffs. Join us for coffee and we'll tell you all about it."

Vanessa was definitely not "kitchen company," and to-

69

gether Diane and Greg led the way into the living room.
"If I had known you had a guest . . ." Vanessa said in an
insinuating tone.

"Diane's not a guest; she's family," Greg interrupted.
"Do you take sugar or cream?" he asked. "It's been so long,
I've forgotten."

"Cream, please." Vanessa ran her tongue over her pale
lips in catlike anticipation of the scene to come. As Greg
left the room, her glance lingered with sardonic amusement
on the turban and robe Diane had draped herself in, and on
her slender bare feet. "This adventure was on the cliffs, did
you say?"

The realization of how all this must look to Lyle's sister
rendered Diane mute. However, Greg heard Vanessa's insinuating question as he returned with a tray of coffee things.
His eyes sharp with warning, he growled, "That's what I
said. We were caught by fog and had to spend the night in
a sort of cave."

Diane saw the flicker of uncertainty in Vanessa's eyes
and heard in her breathy "Oh," a backing down from her
triumphal haughtiness. Glancing around the room, the older
woman changed the subject with a vague "You seem to be
well accommodated here." Then she took a long brown
envelope from her purse and said in her usual brisk tone,
"I brought the papers you asked for, Greg, when you called
me from Paris. I trust you'll find them in order. But if you
have any questions, I'm stopping at the Grand Hotel in
Dinard. Lyle will join me there in a few days." Vanessa
darted a hostile glance Diane's way, then continued, "We
want to look at some property for Kimball Construction.
Lyle and I both think it would be a good idea to enter the
European market for tract homes." Setting her coffee cup
down with a decisive little click against the saucer, Vanessa
rose. "We must get together again, Greg, when Lyle comes."

"Diane and I will hold ourselves in readiness," he answered, imitating her pompously formal tone.

Vanessa swept them both with her cold eyes. "I'm sure,"
she said laconically.

Diane's heart skipped a beat with anxiety. Why had Greg referred to them like that, making it look to Vanessa as though they were a couple?

When Vanessa left, Greg gave Diane a long, appraising stare. "You're afraid of her," he said flatly.

"I can't help it. I've never been intensely disliked the way she dislikes me. I don't know how to handle it. Besides, somehow she always manages to make me feel inferior."

"That doesn't seem like you at all," he mused. Diane shrugged and bent to pick up the serving tray. "She has the power over you."

"The power?" Diane asked.

"Like a witch. Only, you're the one who's given her that power by letting yourself be affected by what she thinks of you."

Diane paused on her way to the kitchen. "You may be right, but I don't seem able to get over it. She's always had that effect on me."

"Vanessa's a bully," he said quietly. "You've got to stand up to her. I found that out when I was a kid."

Resuming her walk to the kitchen, Diane said carelessly, "Ah, but you've had more time to learn how to deal with her than I."

He caught up with her then and took the tray out of her hands, placing it on the kitchen table next to her. "You'll have plenty of time . . . if you marry Lyle."

"There's no *if* about it. I'm *going* to marry Lyle, and when I do I'll try to make friends with Vanessa, not fight her."

He placed his hand gently under her chin and tilted it upward. "It won't work, Diane. Friendship can exist only between equals, and you can't be equal if you're afraid. You've got to fight her at one time or another, the way you do me."

Suddenly, without warning, his hand slid down her neck and between her breasts. He ripped the terry-cloth robe open. The cool air, unexpected, struck her bare flesh like an icy blast. Surprise and shock gave way to outrage. Without thinking, Diane reached down and picked up a cup. She pulled her arm back to hurl it at him, but he stepped away, dodging adroitly as the china smashed into the wall beside him. Hands in his pockets, he leaned nonchalantly against the wall and ran his darkly gleaming eyes slowly over her. Then he grinned. "See what I mean?" he said tauntingly.

Diane didn't deign to answer him. Suddenly aware of her nakedness, she pulled the voluminous robe around her and strode out of the room. *Arrogant, interfering busybody! How dare he do a thing like that to prove his point!* But her anger was only the counterpoint to the thrill that hummed through her body as she recalled how his eyes had promised to rejoice each and every part of her exposed by the opened robe.

Her sore throat now occupied all of Diane's thoughts. She consulted a specialist in Rennes and faithfully followed the regimen of medication and rest he prescribed. On his advice, she stopped practicing and temporarily canceled her lessons with Madame Daudon. Even her morning jogging was prohibited, as well as all excursions in the damp night air.

To keep her spirits up, Diane dwelled on Lyle's imminent arrival in Saint-Cast and the good times they would have together. Inevitably, however, every time she thought of Lyle, her mind strayed to Greg. He was a problem nagging at her for solution, an intruder into her life whom she didn't seem able to keep out, a man who took liberties with her that she didn't mind as much as she should. In short, he was a threat to the well-ordered life she had created for herself, and would have to be warded off.

Therefore, when the phone rang and his deep voice seductively said, "Goddess?" she clamped down hard on the quick leap of her heart.

"Sister-in-law to be," she answered coolly.

"To be or not to be," he quipped dryly. "How's the throat?"

"At the moment, not too good. But I'm taking medicine

and resting, and the doctor I'm seeing in Rennes is optimistic about my recovery by next month."

"Good. I'd hate to think our glorious night together might result in your losing out on the audition."

"I don't see anything glorious about spending the night with a bunch of seagulls and gannets."

"That's what I told Vanessa, but she didn't seem to believe me. Maybe I wasn't convincing enough."

She could hear the repressed chuckle in his voice and it infuriated her. "You wouldn't be trying to break up my engagement by getting me in wrong with Lyle, would you, Greg?" she asked tartly.

"Of course not. Whatever gave you that idea?"

His bland answer wasn't convincing. "I wouldn't put it past you," she retorted.

"Heaven forbid!" he said with mock piety. "Listen, what I called you about is that the Poilvets' plants seem to have been struck by some mysterious ailment and are looking very poorly. I'm afraid *monsieur* and *madame* will be heart-broken when they return and see them. Can you come over and take a look at them?"

"Plants?" Diane said dubiously. "I don't remember any plants."

"Sure. There's a moldy old fern in the hall and something in the kitchen that looks like hemlock, and a man-eating monster on the back porch that the Poilvets undoubtedly used as a guard dog."

Diane laughed in spite of herself. "Maybe you're giving them too much water."

"Or not enough?"

She grew serious then. The Poilvets *would* be upset if their plants died. They were very particular about their pos-sessions. "I'll stop by and look at them when I go out to do my errands," she said decisively. "I've had house plants and know a little something about them."

When she hung up, she glanced in the mirror over the telephone. Her cheeks were flushed, and she could feel the pleasant racing of her heart. All her indignation at Greg had evaporated in the sunny warmth of his humor. Was it wise in such a case to be alone with him in his house again? Her eyes drifted to the phone. She could call him and say she wouldn't be able to come after all. On the other hand, wouldn't such caution be an overreaction? If a Holiday Homes client called, it was her duty to go to the house; and surely she was sophisticated enough to handle any situation that might come up between them. So she peeled off the terry-cloth jumpsuit she wore around the house and changed into a short-sleeved workshirt of bleached indigo chambray and a matching skirt with a white canvas belt. Looking down at her now-tanned shapely legs, she undid the last four snaps of the skirt—a little daring perhaps for Saint-Cast, but the long-awaited Parisians were finally flocking into the small town. She also unbuttoned the shirt to a fashionable depth.

She threw her string shopping bag onto the cracked plastic seat of her aunt's ancient Citroën Deux Chevaux and coaxed the motor into action. The car, which resembled a gray bathtub inverted over four wheels, finally took off in a black cloud of polluting smoke. Diane's first stop was the center of town, where she picked up some needed groceries and returned a few empty wine bottles for the deposit.

Greg's place was next, and it seemed to Diane that her heart was going faster than the little Citroën's engine. Her feelings were as polarized as a magnetic field. One part of her wanted to see Greg again, to watch the flicker of laughter in his eyes, to be close to his big, virile frame and hear his deep, vibrantly warm voice. But the other, rational, side of her repudiated these reactions, and dismissed the physical attraction as sure to vanish once Lyle arrived.

Diane stopped the car at the Poilvet house. She redid her shirt up to the top button and snapped her skirt so that it covered her thighs. Then she got out.

"It's the plant doctor," she said when Greg opened the door to her ring.

"Come on in, Doc, I've got the patients all lined up for you."

Diane saw that this was the indeed the case. A browning

fern, a puny-looking dieffenbachia, and a dusty dracaena stood side by side in pots in the foyer.

"Stick out your tongues for the doctor, fellers," Greg said.

Diane looked the plants over. "I'm not sure this warranted a house call."

"Money's no object, Doc. What've they got?"

"Well, from the looks of them, I'd say the fern's not been getting enough water, the dieffenbachia's been getting too much, and the dracaena needs her leaves syringed." She turned to Greg and fixed him with a stern look. "Have you been feeding them?"

"Only a little chicken soup."

"The grocery in town carries plant food. The directions are on the box." She turned to go.

"How much do I owe you, Doc?" he asked softly.

Going along with the joke, she raised one supercilious eyebrow and said, "Nothing, it's part of the Holiday Homes service."

"But I insist on paying," he said persuasively. He took a step toward her, to where she stood with her hand on the door. One strong hand swept her hair up over her ear and held it there. The other rested gently on her sculptured cheek. Then he traced the convoluted shell of her ear with his lips, filling it with his warm breath, while she stood with her eyes closed, spellbound by the subtle, almost pastel, sensation of pleasure he was giving her.

His big hand, gentle on her face, turned her toward him.

"Look at me, Diane. I don't want you thinking of someone else."

His command was a stone thrown into a pool. A ripple of uneasiness ran through her. He wanted her more aware than she wished to be.

Stubbornly, she kept her eyes closed, and the long, dark lashes swept her flushed cheeks.

He kissed each full eyelid. Then he said, "Open them. Look at me, Diane."

Meeting his gaze, she thrilled to the passionate tenderness

she saw there. Everything about him emanated the warmth and life she longed for.

He folded her in his arms. "Oh, Diane, my dearest," he murmured. "How can I give you up?" He tightened his embrace, ravaging her lips and her face and her neck with kisses that exploded like dynamite. Feverishly, he undid the top button of her shirt and continued until her soft, billowing breasts lay under his hands. His mouth astride hers in a long, pulsing kiss, his fingers caressed the straining breasts in motions that made her nerves sing with excitement, like high-tension wires.

She felt herself relentlessly drawn to him. The very cells of her body were pulled toward his. Deep within her, a terrible wanting wrenched at her resolve to resist him. She desired him so savagely that she had to dig her nails into her palms to keep herself from touching him. With an effort hard as pain, Diane pushed him way.

"No, Greg!" she cried. "No! This is wrong. Leave me alone." She turned to the door, buttoning her blouse as she went.

The phone rang and, still confused by what had just happened, Diane obeyed her first impulse. She took a few steps, picked up the receiver, and said "Hello?"

Then, absently, she pulled the still-open portion of the shirt around her.

"This is Vanessa, Diane," the cold, dry voice at the other end of the line announced. "Will you put Greg on, please . . . if he's in a condition to come to the phone."

Wordlessly, Diane extended the receiver to Greg. He took it with a sharp look at her. She turned her back and closed her ears to his voice. Emotionally upset, she fumbled with the buttons of her shirt. Finally, she was ready to leave, but with her hand on the doorknob, Greg stopped her.

"What's wrong, Diane? What do you care what Vanessa thinks?"

"You set me up," she said bitterly. "You knew she would call this afternoon about some business matter you two have going. That's why you got me over here on that phony pretext about the plants. You're despicable, Greg Kimball."

She turned the knob, but his big hand was on her wrist, preventing her from opening the door.

"I wouldn't do a thing like that and you know it," he said roughly. "You're scared silly of that bitch. You couldn't even talk to her on the phone just now. So what if you were here with me, that's none of her business, is it?"

She looked at him for a long time. Then realization burst on her like a shaft of light in a dark room. He was right. Vanessa was definitely not her keeper; neither, for that matter, was Lyle or Greg. She was her own woman. A feeling of tremendous freedom, as of a great weight suddenly removed, followed this insight. Diane raised her eyebrows in further speculation. Moreover, she shouldn't allow Vanessa to make her feel defensive about being at Greg's. Granted, there was a strong physical pull between herself and this attractive man standing before her, but that was natural considering her years of sexual abstinence and the fact that they liked each other and enjoyed one another's company. What was more, except for a few kisses, she and Greg had managed to resist this attraction. She might even tell Lyle about it, so that they would begin their life together with scrupulous honesty.

All the while Greg was watching her as though trying to assess her reaction to what he had said. Now she returned his searching look. A new aspect of Greg Kimball had been opened up to her—that of an intimately perceptive friend.

"You're right, Greg, but my knowing it doesn't change anything. Maybe it all comes from my mother, who used to do dressmaking and alterations for Vanessa and the other 'ladies' of Forestville. She was always excessively polite to them; after all, they were our only livelihood. She instilled this—I hate to say subservience, but maybe that's what it was—in me when they used to come to our house for fittings. So even though I know it's wrong and I fight against the feeling, I can't help but treat Vanessa as if she were a vastly superior being."

Greg chuckled. "All of which suits Vanessa to a T, of

course. The little luncheon I've planned should give you
practice in how to rebel against a queen."

"Luncheon?"

"Didn't you hear me invite Vanessa here for lunch tomorrow?" Diane shook her head. "She's coming at one. I
mentioned that you might come, too. It'll be that family
get-together we've been talking about," Greg added with a
grin.

In spite of her brave thoughts, lunch in Greg's house
with the sharp-tongued Vanessa was an alarming prospect
to Diane. "I have . . ."

"No music lesson; you've already told me that," Greg
interrupted. "And therefore, no excuse. Right?"

"What are you going to do for food?" Diane asked. "Will
you cook?"

"Not for company. I'm going to use the *charcuterie* in
town. My mouth waters every time I pass those plump brown
chickens turning on the spit in the window."

"So does mine," Diane confessed with a laugh. "Is there
anything I can bring?" she asked.

"Just your beautiful self," Greg said huskily.

At twelve the next day, Diane stood in front of the full-
length mirror in her bedroom and made a face. She hated
the dress she had on. It was one of her mistakes—a shirt
dress in royal, aqua, and fuchsia stripes that she had bought
merely because it was polyester jersey and would pack well.
But its long sleeves and length made it the only dress in her
wardrobe conservative enough for a lunch with Vanessa.
So with a sigh she left the mirror and went to find the woven
straw handbag she planned to carry. Everything but white
gloves, she thought with a grimace.

When the doorbell rang, she was surprised to see Greg
on the threshold.

"Why aren't you home slaving over a hot stove, or at
least unwrapping salami?" she asked.

Instead of answering, he stood looking at her as if at a
refrigerator full of four-day-old fish.

"I thought so," he said grimly. "That's why I came over, busy as I am with decorations and food," he added in a high, fluty voice.

"What's wrong? I'm standing here in my famous-name bra, maybe?"

"You'd look better if you were. Come on, I don't have much time." With that, he brushed past her, into the house. "Where's your bedroom?"

"Upstairs," she said, totally mystified. When they were both standing in the middle of the room, she asked sharply, "Do you mind telling me what's going on?"

"What's coming off is more like it. Where did you get that rag? It's the only ugly outfit I've ever seen on you." He shook his head sadly. "I knew you'd dress for Vanessa instead of yourself. Take it off; I'll find something else for you to wear."

"No, you won't! Stop meddling in my life, Greg."

He turned around on his way to the closet. "I don't have much time, Diane," he repeated warningly.

"Then go back to your table decorations and broiled chicken. I chose this dress, and I'm going to wear it." She stood with her hands on her hips, glaring at him defiantly.

"Like hell you are. I won't let you do this to yourself."

With one long step, he was in front of her. Grasping her by the shoulder, he quickly undid the top two buttons of the dress. She thrust his hand away, but it returned to work on the third button. Whether he intended it or not, the motions of his hand against her breast were arousing her desire for him. At the same time, she resented his taking control in this way. She began to pummel his broad chest with her fists, but he grasped her wrists and held them in a viselike grip.

Laughing, he tumbled her backward onto the bed and, kneeling over her, pinned her shoulders down. "You're a real tiger, aren't you?" he said admiringly. "If you showed half that spunk with Vanessa, you'd have her jumping through hoops for you." His voice became serious then. "But I want you out of that dress if I have to take it off you myself."

He moved his hand over her breasts, covered now by only
the sheer net of her bra, across her flat stomach, and slowly
down to the last button. An anticipatory thrill coursed slowly
through Diane like the long climb of a roller coaster. From
the look in Greg's eyes, it was evident that only a word or
gesture from her would suffice to plunge them both into a
maelstrom of passion. "Who's doing it, Diane, you or me?"
he asked in a voice rough with repressed desire.

"I'll take it off," she said quietly.

He let her up and got up himself to return to the closet.
She stood in her creamy satin half-slip, stockings, and black
patent-leather pumps, and waited while he rummaged among
her clothes. When he faced her again, she turned her head,
suddenly shy before that look in his eyes of mingled admiration and desire.

"Here, put this on," he said huskily. "This is you." He
handed her a sleeveless black cotton frock with a peplum
and a black and white checkered sash.

Diane slipped the dress over her head and wrapped the
sash around her waist, finishing it off with a big bow in
front. The dress had a plunging V that she herself had
modified with an invisible snap so that she might wear it
in the daytime as well as for evening. She closed the snap
now and walked to the mirror to look at herself. There was
no question that this dress was infinitely more attractive
than the other.

In the mirror, she saw Greg behind her, his brown eyes
glinting with amusement. Then she felt his hands under her
arms and around her breasts. He released the snap, and the
dress fell open to her smooth tanned skin and more than a
hint of cleavage.

She turned quickly. "I can't wear it like that to your
luncheon."

"Consider it a flag of independence and wear it," he
counseled.

"All right," she said reluctantly. She turned to the mirror
again. "But my hair!" she wailed, pushing at the burnished
gold waves that, in the struggle, had escaped from the smooth

coif she had tamed them into. "I look like a wild woman."

Standing behind her, he pulled her against him and buried his face in the thick tawny tresses. Then he gently tugged at her ear with his teeth. When he let go, he whispered seductively, "You don't know it yet, but that's what you are, Diane."

As she started off a little later for lunch with her future sister-in-law, Diane thought she had never been so unready for a social event. The parts of her body that had known Greg's experienced hands were still imprinted with the thrill of his touch. And she couldn't stop thinking of him. Although his meddling was infuriating, she was also touched by his interest in her as a person. Her father had been almost nonexistent in her life. Mike had been the sun, and she only a pale planet beside him. And Lyle was rather inclined to let matters rest as he found them. But Greg was a man who both cared and acted.

When she arrived at Greg's house, Vanessa was already there, cool and impeccable in a beige linen suit. She stared pointedly at the deep V in the black dress, but to Diane's surprise, she found herself amused rather than mortified by Vanessa's attitude. Released from the inhibiting effects of shame and helpless anger, she was able to direct an equally penetrating glance at the prissy bow that closed Vanessa's blouse high on her neck.

Diane was pleased by the elegance with which Greg had set the table, even to a bowl of beautifully arranged wild flowers in the center. And she raised her eyebrows at the dishes he had arranged on the buffet. He must have cleaned out the *charcuterie,* she thought, as she surveyed the platters of sliced chicken and ham, an assortment of patés, a kaleidoscope of garnished vegetable salads, and a plate of *bouchées à la reine,* which were patty shells filled with a creamed seafood mixture and called literally "mouthfuls for a queen" because they had been invented for the wife of Louis XV.

Conversation was mostly about general subjects—what was to be seen in Brittany and what was new in Forestville.

Vanessa made a few references to her and Lyle's plans to build tract homes in northern France and to Lyle's imminent arrival. Every time she mentioned Lyle, she impaled Diane with a warning or hostile glance.

Finally tiring of these attacks, Diane said forthrightly, "I'm looking forward to seeing Lyle again, both for his sake and mine. I think he'll be pleased when I tell him Greg and I have become friends."

Not entirely the truth at the present moment perhaps, but it would be the truth once Lyle had arrived.

Lunch over, Vanessa left and Diane helped Greg clear the table.

"How does it feel to slay a dragon?" he asked slyly, a plate of leftovers in each hand.

"Vanessa?"

He nodded. "I saw how you handled her. You did well, Diane."

"Thanks to you," she admitted honestly.

When they reached the kitchen, he handed her a bottle of detergent. "If you'll fill the sink with soapy water, I'll scrape the plates and hand them to you."

Diane watched, horrified, as he proceeded to tilt the leftover food into a tall white-enameled pail with small holes in the raised lid.

"That's for bread—not garbage!" she exclaimed. "The French put the *baguettes,* the long loaves, in those pails."

They both stared helplessly down at the pail for a moment; then they burst into peals of laughter. They shared their merriment with their eyes, but it wouldn't have taken much, Diane thought, for that hilarious moment to bring them together in a loving embrace.

Greg must have seen it, too; for when they recovered, he said in a low, urgent voice, "Don't go to Lyle when he comes, Diane. You may think it's a little soon to tell about us, but it's not too soon to know he's not the man for you."

Diane could only stare at him for a moment. Put in words

like that, with Lyle due to arrive any day, what Greg was proposing alarmed her.

"Don't talk like that, Greg," she finally said. "When Lyle comes, everything will be different. You'll see."

He gave her a long, sardonic look. "I think you're in for a surprise, Diane."

# - *8* -

TWO DAYS LATER, Lyle called. He was at the Dinard airport. Would it be convenient for Diane to pick him up? If not, he would take a taxi.

"'Convenient' isn't the word," Diane answered. "I'm dying to see you. I'll be there in half an hour at the longest."

With an unerring instinct for the ultimate dramatic gesture, her aunt's little Citroën absolutely refused to start. After the last futile try, Diane turned the ignition off and thought about her life. Aside from the fact that she was a singer with a bad throat, an engaged woman attracted to another man, and heiress to a car with all the reliability of a flea, she didn't have a trouble in the world.

She got out and gave the old heap a sour look. Then she looked down at her shoes. They were strong enough. She aimed a kick at the fender and called the car a very strong insult in French. Feeling better, she walked back into the house.

What to do? A taxi to the airport would cost a fortune. Vanessa didn't have a car. That left only Greg. With a fatalistic shrug, Diane went to the telephone. Even grand opera didn't have a plot in which the heroine went to meet her fiancé with his half-brother, to whom the lady in question was devastatingly attracted.

But her misgivings were obviously not shared by Greg. He was beaming with happiness when he arrived to pick her up. Moreover, instead of the usual T-shirt and chinos, he wore a handsome brown and white striped seersucker suit with a pima-cotton button-down shirt in tan, and a jaunty salmon-colored bow tie.

Diane glanced down at her own simple navy-blue linen blazer, blouse, and skirt. "You didn't have to dress!" she said.

"I didn't—for Lyle. I have to go to Grenoble for a couple of days." He nodded toward his car. "I've got my bag in the trunk."

Diane glanced at him suspiciously. True, when they first met he had mentioned his intention of using Saint-Cast as home base for various business trips, but he hadn't done any traveling since then that she was aware of. Why was he leaving now? And why was he in such high good humor?

During the drive to the airport, she kept stealing glances at him, trying to fathom his feelings. He didn't seem curious about how she felt about seeing Lyle again. He displayed no symptom of jealousy. He was as calmly confident as a man driving his wife to meet an old friend.

Maybe he was through with her, Diane thought. He had come on to her strong while Lyle was absent. Now that Lyle would be here in Saint-Cast, Greg, like any sensible man, was going to give up trying to get what he couldn't have.

Yet Diane felt bruised and angry. Greg had been only using her. Perhaps he had been trying to get back at his brother for some past injury. More likely, he was just look-ing for a little midsummer diversion. With her temper at the simmering point, she had little to say during the ride. However, Greg's maddening serenity seemed to make him impervious to her mood.

They walked into the neat, modern air terminal together. Diane saw Lyle immediately, standing slim and elegant beside his fine leather bags. She ran across the tile floor to him, the quick tapping of her heels followed by Greg's quieter tread.

Diane threw her arms around Lyle's neck and raised her face for his kiss. As his lips came down to hers, she was suddenly seized by a longing for Greg's mouth instead, for the warm ardor of his lips pressing sweet, wild kisses on forbidden, intimate places. A shiver of apprehension went through her. Was this the surprise Greg had said she would have when Lyle arrived—the knowledge that she had chosen the wrong man?

She turned toward Greg and met his steady gaze. He was studying her through half-narrowed eyes, and Diane concluded from his smug expression that he had guessed her feelings. Her whole being blazed up in anger at him. She hated him for having a hold on her and knowing it. And she resolved to break that hold. Now that Lyle was here, it should be easy. After all, he *was* the man she was engaged to.

Putting her hand on Lyle's arm, Diane explained casually, "Aunt Yvonne's car wouldn't start, so Greg drove me."

The brothers shook hands, then Greg said, "Here, let me help you," and picked up one of the bags. The three of them started to walk out of the terminal together, when Lyle stopped short. "Listen, would you mind if I grabbed a bite here at the airport? I didn't have time to eat before my plane left London."

"It's all right with me," Greg answered. "I'm on my way to Grenoble, but it won't make any difference if I get there an hour later. Besides, I'd like to talk to you before I leave."

"Okay with you, Diane?" Lyle asked.

Diane thought fast. The smirk on Greg's face was maddening. She didn't think she could stand an hour in his and Lyle's company without exploding into anger at him. So she put her hand on Lyle's arm again and said pointedly, "There's a nice little restaurant in the terminal, but most of the tables are for two."

As Lyle stared at Diane, obviously surprised at her bad manners, Greg said blithely, "That's all right. I'll just pull up another chair."

Throughout lunch, Diane avoided looking at Greg. When she occasionally did, his obvious satisfaction at her distress exacerbated her anger so that she ended up addressing all her remarks to Lyle and responding only to what he, and not Greg, had to say. Too late, she realized that she was making a serious mistake. Lyle's blue eyes rested on her face in a constant questioning look, while Greg began more and more to have an air of the cat who had swallowed the cream. She tried to make up for the attention her discourtesy was arousing by asking Greg some banal question, but the words stuck in her throat.

When they rose from the table, it was Greg who held her blazer for her. Feeling his hands on her shoulders, she went rigid and lashed out without thinking, "I'll put it on myself, thank you."

Turning, she looked full into Lyle's face. His lips were pursed in a silent whistle and there was a shrewd look in his eyes.

Greg left them in the parking lot of the air terminal and got into his rented fire-engine-red Renault. He raised his hand in a breezy wave as he drove off, but the expression in his sable eyes was inscrutable as he watched Diane move close to Lyle and slip her arm through his.

During the next few days, Diane debated whether she should tell Lyle that she had been attracted to Greg and had even thought she might be falling in love with him but that it was all over now. She decided not to. Although he might have guessed that there had been more between her and Greg than a family relationship, Diane thought that it would embarrass Lyle to hear about it from her. Besides, it would all be for nothing anyway since her involvement with Greg was finished and she had regained her grip on herself.

Diane found herself appreciating Lyle's steady, quiet affection and tried hard not to compare the two brothers. If Lyle wasn't as vibrant a person as Greg, that was all right. She had had enough highly charged emotion in her life; she was ready for a safe harbor.

One evening when she and Lyle were in the restaurant of the Grand Hotel in Dinard, Lyle said, "Vanessa and I will need a translator as we go around Brittany looking at property and talking to real-estate agents. Vanessa's French is practically nonexistent, and mine isn't good enough for the job. It's a lot to ask, but would you be able to go with us?"

Diane hesitated. She hated to turn Lyle down in something so important to him, but she had seen her doctor only the day before and had received bad news.

"I wish I could, but my throat's not getting better fast enough for the audition, and the doctor insists that I rest more. I'm afraid driving around with you and Vanessa might retard my recovery. I'm sorry, Lyle, but I can't chance it. That audition is just too important to me."

He quickly covered her hand with his in a gesture of sympathy. "I understand, hon. You stay here and take care of your throat. That's more important. But perhaps you could recommend someone else?"

Diane's gray eyes gleamed with an idea. "I think I have the very person for you, a friend of mine named Nadine Kerbellec. She and her brother Guy are folk singers. They've just come back to Saint-Cast after playing an engagement in Quiberon. I know she's free because she called me up last night to tell me she was bored silly in Saint-Cast and could hardly wait to start at a club in Paris in a couple of weeks." Since Lyle looked doubtful, Diane continued in a persuasive voice, "She's a charming woman and she knows Brittany better than anyone else except possibly her brother."

"Does she speak English?"

"Not fluently, but well enough for your purpose, I should think."

"Well, call her, then, Diane. Ask if she'd be interested. We'll pay her, of course."

His blue eyes searched Diane's clear gray ones. "I'm sorry it won't be you who's going with us."

"I am too," she said regretfully.

He ran his hand over her wavy red-gold hair. "I think perhaps we've been apart too much. Don't you agree, Diane?"

She caught his hand and held it in both of hers. "We won't always be, Lyle dear." However, even as she spoke, she wondered about these words of reassurance. During all their separations, she had never missed Lyle the way she missed Greg now.

She would enter a room where there were people and think for a minute that he was there. Once or twice she fancied that she saw him on the beach. And always there was a sharp pang of disappointment when she realized that the person she'd seen wasn't Greg. Their times together, though few, had left an aching void inside her. What hurt the most was the thought that he hadn't really cared about her. If he had cared, he wouldn't have been so nonchalant about Lyle's arrival in Saint-Cast.

When Diane described Lyle's offer over the phone, Nadia accepted enthusiastically. "Don't you want to meet Lyle first?" Diane asked. "You'll be in rather close contact with him for quite a while."

"If he's your fiancé, Diane, he must be a very fine fellow."

"His older sister can be difficult at times."

"I live with *Maman,*" Nadia said with meaningful simplicity.

Diane smiled. Nadia wanted nothing so much as her own apartment in Rennes, but Madame Kerbellec wouldn't hear of it. Very few people, and certainly not Nadia, crossed Madame Kerbellec.

"Even so, I think you all should meet. I've wanted you and Lyle to get to know each other anyway, so why don't you come to my house for lunch tomorrow and I'll have Lyle and Vanessa there. That way, they'll be able to explain their project to you."

Vanessa, not unexpectedly, refused Diane's invitation, but Lyle came, looking handsome and suave in a yellow knit polo shirt with a deep-blue ascot and creamy flannel slacks. By chance, Nadine arrived wearing almost the same ensemble—a buttercup-yellow knit top with a straight white cotton skirt and a nautical-looking navy scarf around her neck.

The similarity in dress broke the ice between them, and the shy Nadia was soon laughing up into Lyle's face as he joked about his clothes looking better on her than on him. Watching them, Diane was struck by what had never occurred to her before. Regardless of their difference in coloring, they resembled each other. Both had a spare, etched look that derived from their rather sharp facial features and their narrow, straight bodies. Nadia even had the boyish form of a twenties flapper.

It was also obvious that they would get on together. Lyle's courteous attentiveness was drawing Nadia out. Gaining courage, she began to sparkle with the pleasure of good conversation. Her dark eyes snapped with glee when Lyle told a funny story, and expressions crossed her mobile face as quickly as clouds scudded over the Breton sky.

It didn't matter what Vanessa might think of Nadia; Lyle was obviously delighted with her. He asked Diane for a map of Brittany, and soon two neatly shaped heads, one dark and one blond, were bent over it. They would start the very next day, Lyle decided. They would get all their investigating done during this one trip, staying in hotels and inns wherever they found themselves instead of driving back to Saint-Cast each day. "That way," he told Diane, "I'll be able to go to Nice with you and stay while you audition. Then we can have a holiday—go to Monte Carlo, if you like, or Antibes."

With suspicious precision, Greg called the day after Lyle, Nadia, and Vanessa left.

"Goddess?" he drawled. "I just got back, and you'll never guess what I found in the house."

*A rattlesnake, I hope, all coiled up and ready to strike. Coffee laced with poison. Quicklime in the bathtub.*

"I never play guessing games," she answered coolly, "so why don't you tell me? But whatever it is, I'm not going over to look at it."

"Holiday Homes will hear about this dereliction of duty, young lady," he said in stentorian tones.

Instead of bantering with him as he obviously wished, Diane replied seriously, "Let them. I couldn't care less."

His voice grave now, Greg said, "What's wrong, Diane? You're not still upset over whatever was bothering you when we met Lyle, are you?"

His bland hypocrisy infuriated her. Choked with rage, she answered, "What kind of a woman do you think I am, Greg? Do you really think you can move in when Lyle is gone, as I'm sure you know he is now, have a little fun with me, and then move out when he comes back?"

"Diane! What are you saying? I never thought such a thing."

"All I know is you were happy as a lark when we met Lyle, and as soon as Lyle leaves you're back with that same old stupid ploy about there being something wrong at the house."

"I'm coming over, Diane," he said firmly. "And when I do, you'd better let me in."

Diane slammed the receiver down and, grabbing her purse off the top of the piano, strode to the door. Her car was out of the question. It was running again, but Diane never knew when or where it might leave her stranded. The town was too small; Greg could find her there. But the beach was crowded with summer visitors now.

She rented a blue and white striped tent from the concessionaire. Then, plowing through the sand in high-heeled pumps and ignoring the stares of the crowd uniformly attired in swimsuits, she followed the boy who carried it to the end of the line of beach tents. But once ensconced inside the tent, she had nothing to do. In her hurry to leave the house, she hadn't thought to pick up a book. So, pillowing her head on her handbag, she curled herself into a ball, like a hedgehog hiding from a predator, she thought, and tried to go to sleep. But doubt began to assail her. Should she have stayed and faced up to Greg? she wondered. Wouldn't that have been a more successful means of putting an end to his pursuit of her than running away? Now he might simply continue to play his dangerous games with her. And yet . . . and yet . . . somehow she couldn't square the caddish behavior she had just accused him of with her other knowledge of him.

Eventually, the sound of the sea and the sun's warmth seeping through the canvas tent put her to sleep. She wanted to sleep, as an escape from problems she didn't seem able to solve, and when she felt a light touch on her leg, she pushed the consciousness of it away. But the touch turned into a hand laid firmly on her knee, and she admitted its reality by opening her eyes.

Greg was squatting beside her, a look of concern on his face. "Why did you leave? I asked you to stay and wait for me."

"It's pretty obvious, isn't it? I didn't want to see you."

"Is it the same old problem, Diane?" he asked quietly. "The eternal male who loves 'em and leaves 'em for somebody else?"

She sat up then, pulling her dress down so it covered her and crossing her arms over her knees. "You've got it wrong. It's the eternal male who doesn't love them and won't leave them alone, the man who uses them as it suits his convenience."

His voice ringing with emotion, he said, "I wasn't using you, Diane. If I seemed carefree and happy at the airport, it was because I've known since I met you that I was the man for you, not Lyle, and because I was confident that with Lyle here you would find that out very quickly. That was the surprise I said lay in store for you, the realization that you're engaged to the wrong man. When I came back today, I didn't know that Lyle was gone until you told me.

I know you're not the kind of woman to play around with two men at a time, nor am I moving in on Lyle. I'd be doing him no kindness to let him marry a woman who doesn't love him. You love me, Diane, whether you'll admit it or not, and I love you."

Diane averted her eyes from his steady, compelling gaze and compressed her lips. It was like pain, she thought: if you ignored it, it might go away. She didn't want to know that he loved her; she didn't want to love him. The man she wanted to love was the man to whom she was engaged.

As if he could read her thoughts, Greg said, "Don't be afraid of rocking the boat you and Lyle are in. It's only a canvas backdrop anyway, the kind in which people at sea-side resorts have their pictures taken."

Diane had a sudden image of herself and Lyle seated in a cardboard motor boat, happy smiles pasted on their faces. It was like all the smiling pictures of Mike and her in the local newspaper—"Popular Forestville Couple at Charity Ball" . . . "Mike and Diane James Find Good Buys at Benson Hospital Bazaar"—taken after she had found out about Mike's infidelities, taken when her heart was breaking. Greg was right. If she married Lyle, it would be the second time around for her of a life without love. She felt gratitude, affection, and friendship for Lyle—but not the kind of love a man and a woman should have for each other, the kind of love, she now admitted to herself, that she and Greg had.

The sun was beating mercilessly down on the tent. Diane wiped perspiration from her forehead and felt a trickle of sweat from her armpit run down her side. Greg's business shirt was wet, too.

Diane was also aware of a sudden silence around the tent. The steady undercurrent of French conversation had ceased. The piping voice of a child who came to the neighboring tent to ask for his sand pail was abruptly shushed.

In the midst of her anger, sadness, and emotional turmoil, Diane's sense of humor surfaced, buoyant as a cork in deep water. Undoubtedly, the French were listening to this fascinating lovers' quarrel carried on in American English. It was as good as television, which in France had only three channels anyway.

Diane smiled and Greg smiled back at her, his face lit with tenderness. How could she, Diane thought, deny not only herself but Greg the love that was their due? Some people spent their whole lives looking for love and never finding it. It would be wrong not to seize the good fortune that was theirs, the luck to love and be loved.

A tremendous feeling of joy surged up within her like a life-giving fountain, and she said, "I do love you, Greg."

He grinned and shook his head in mock wonder. "I never thought I'd get you to see it."

"You've got a slow learner on your hands, that's all," she said blithely.

"Then let's speed things up." He bent forward to kiss her and toppled them both backward on the sand.

Sand seemed to be everywhere—in her hair; on her cheeks, sticky with sweat; and on the lips he pressed against hers. It was the grittiest, harshest, sweetest kiss he had ever given her. She closed her eyes for it and ran her hands across his broad shoulders just to know he was there. His cotton shirt stuck to his back with perspiration. She loosened his tie and slid her hand under his shirt to be as close to him as she could, to feel his warm skin, to show her love with a caress.

His lips left hers then, and he whispered in her ear, "So you'll tell Lyle about us, soon?"

She whispered back, "Yes."

A few kisses later, Greg said, "I don't know about you, but I'm beginning to learn what a fried egg feels like."

Diane giggled. "Adam and Eve on a raft, that's us."

"What does that mean?"

"An order of bacon and eggs. Didn't I tell you I was a waitress once?"

He nuzzled her neck, leaving a trail of sand on her soft skin. "There are a lot of things I can't wait to find out about you."

When they left the tent, hand in hand, not one in the row of blue and white beach tents was occupied. More Frenchmen sunned themselves, played catch, and built sand castles with their children than had ever before been seen in Saint-Cast.

"Do you have the feeling somehow that we're being watched?" Diane asked.

"I can't imagine why," Greg answered smoothly. "I told the concessionaire when I came looking for you that you were a famous star of American television who couldn't stand the nudity of Saint-Tropez and that I had a rare skin disease that turned me the color of Dijon mustard in the sun."

What had seemed easy that afternoon on the beach became harder to envision doing as the time for Lyle's return to Saint-Cast approached. Diane was plagued by memories of his kindness during Mike's illness. His own sweet nature caused her to dread hurting him. Ending her commitment to him, even though he had left their engagement open-ended, made her feel guilty. Her mind constantly rehearsed the scene that had to be played, but it never seemed to come out right. Yet she reminded herself that she would be doing him a greater injury if she didn't tell him.

The only question was, when and where? Nothing would really soften the blow, but a dinner cooked by her own hands would at least show how much she cared about him. So she started thinking about menus and washed Aunt Yvonne's good china and polished her few pieces of silver in preparation. Candles were out, she decided; too romantic. Wine, of course, but no drinks before or after. After a snifter or two of Calvados, even Lyle might reveal a side she had never seen.

When Lyle called to tell her he was back, she held the invitation in abeyance while he answered her questions about the trip. But when he asked if he could see her right away, there was such urgency in his voice that she couldn't refuse him. And, unwilling to let him believe even a day longer than necessary that their relationship was the same as always, Diane decided to break the engagement that very day.

She paced the front room nervously, waiting for him to come. She ran over in her mind all the things she would say to soften the impact of her announcement. Her heart beat painfully fast. She was so fond of Lyle, she didn't think she could stand his reaction when she told him that it was Greg whom she loved. When she glanced out the window and saw him on the front walk, his face hidden by a paper cornucopia of flowers, she felt an added pang of contrition.

To forestall a kiss, when she opened the door she held her arms out for the flowers, saying with a laugh, "Not all for me!"

"Nadia told me you like roses."

"They're my favorite flower," Diane admitted. "Come into the kitchen, why don't you, while I arrange them." She hadn't had to worry about a kiss, she reflected. He had been as adroit as she in avoiding one.

He stood watching her as she snipped the ends of the rose stems with her aunt's kitchen shears, then filled two tall glass vases with water. All the while she practiced mentally how she would begin. She glanced at him once, slim and straight, his eyes serious, and almost wished she didn't love someone else. Life with Lyle had promised to be so easy. But most of all she didn't want to hurt him.

"Lyle," she started tentatively, "there's something I must tell you."

"I've got something to tell you, too."

"You go first," Diane said impulsively.

Lyle gave her a courteous half-bow. "No, you."

Nervously, she stuck a few more of the roses into a vase haphazardly, then turned and faced him. "I can't marry you, Lyle," she said quietly. "I'm in love with Greg."

Diane watched in amazement as a broad smile slowly spread over Lyle's face. When he actually laughed, she felt a little hurt.

"I'm glad you're taking it so well," she said tartly.

His eyes were streaming now, and he was laughing so

hard he could hardly talk. "You don't know the half of it, Diane."

"I guess I don't know *any* of it. How about letting me in on the joke?"

He stopped laughing then, but his eyes shone with amusement and a smile still hovered about his lips. "I came here to tell *you* we would have to call the engagement off."

It took a moment for this to sink in, then Diane exploded in a long, joyous peal. They laughed together for a long time, until Diane threw her arms around Lyle's neck and kissed him soundly on the cheek. She drew away then and faced him squarely. "But what . . . ?" she began.

"What made me decide?" he interrupted. "Well, I had an inkling there was something between you and Greg when I saw how angry you were with him at the airport. You never got angry with *me*, Diane. But it wasn't just that. It was something else, something . . ." He began to flounder then, and Diane murmured an encouraging "Yes?"

"I've fallen in love, Diane. I mean, really in love. You and I did love each other, I suppose, but only in a certain sense."

"It was affection, don't you think, Lyle? There's a difference."

Lyle nodded soberly. "A world of difference. I thought you and I could have a happy marriage with what we felt for each other. And perhaps we could have. But this . . . what I feel now . . . seems inevitable and necessary, not . . . well, just comfortable, I suppose one could say."

"I understand, Lyle," Diane said tenderly. "Friendship really isn't enough to build a marriage on. It takes love—genuine, full-bodied, committed love." Then, briskly, she asked, "But who's the lucky girl? You still haven't told me."

"Nadia," he said simply.

"Of course, I should have known," Diane breathed.

"She's felt very badly about what she calls stealing me away from you. Wait till I tell her this!" Lyle looked at the roses still lying on the drain board. "Hey, those are going to be dead before you get them in water." He took a few and Diane took others, and together they arranged the long-stemmed beauties in the two vases. "We owe our happiness to you," Lyle said a little shyly. "It was your idea that Nadia do the translating for Vanessa and me. We were together practically all the time, and . . . it just happened. That old midsummer magic, I guess."

"Vanessa! Does she know?"

Lyle raised his blond eyebrows and rolled his eyes comically. "She's mad as a hornet; keeps talking about there never having been a 'foreign influence,' as she puts it, in our blood line. Of course, she's overlooking the Illini Indian chief, a certain French fur trapper, a Hungarian miner's daughter, and so on. Anyway, she's going home in a huff and leaving me to conclude the final arrangements for the property we'll buy here. But if I know Van, she'll come back for the wedding. Vanessa's bark is a lot worse than her bite."

Diane looked dubious at that, but Vanessa was the least interesting of all the people in this new situation. "The wedding?" she repeated.

Lyle nodded. "Nadia wants to be married in the church in Saint-Cast, the one with the model of a ship hanging in the nave. We haven't set a date yet, but it'll almost surely be in September. I should be finished with my real-estate deals by then. That will be after your audition. You'll come, won't you?"

"Just try to keep me away!" She put her hands to her face and smiled. "I still can't take it all in. Nadia and you."

Lyle grinned foolishly and happily. Then his eyes searched hers. "And Greg and you. When will *that* happy event take place?"

Diane looked puzzled for a moment. "Oh, you mean a wedding." She turned her head slightly, then looked back at him. "I really don't know."

# - *9* -

"DID YOU TELL HIM?" Greg rested his lean hands on the steering wheel and looked at Diane.

She laughed and shook her head. "He told *me*."

"What do you mean?"

"He and Nadine Kerbellec have fallen in love. They're going to be married."

Greg let out a long, sibilant whistle. "That was fast!"

"I believe it's called love at first sight," she said impishly. They studied each other for a long moment, gray eyes and dark ones searching for meanings in a new situation. "But I can't stay in Brittany," Diane added quietly. "My doctor has tried everything, and my voice still hasn't come back. He thinks the warm weather in the south of France is what I need. And if *that* doesn't do it, there's a famous throat specialist in Nice whose name he's given me. I've already arranged with Yann to replace me with Holiday Homes sooner than we had planned." Noting Greg's glum expression, she added pleadingly, "I have to go, Greg. I have to pass that audition."

His brown hands whitened as he gripped the wheel hard. "I understand. When are you leaving?"

"Tomorrow," she said sadly. "It'll take me two days to reach the Riviera."

"You're not driving that old wreck of your aunt's!" Greg said, shocked.

"Do you have any idea what train and air fare are these days?"

"I'll drive you," Greg said firmly.

"Can you take the time off? I thought there were various plants you wanted to visit."

"My time's pretty much my own. It's settled," he added, backing the Renault out of the driveway, and Diane thought it best not to argue with that granite jaw. Then Greg's face softened. "I understand the marriage room in the city hall of Menton is famous for its Cocteau frescoes. Menton can't be far from Nice."

"Twenty miles at the most."

"Well, how about it?" His dark eyes were luminous with love as he looked at her.

"Is that a proposal?"

He grinned rather sheepishly. "I meant to wait for a more romantic time and place, Diane, but with you patience isn't my long suit. Put in formal terms, will you, Diane James, marry me, Gregory Kimball? I can't go down on bended knee, there isn't room in the Renault. But as soon as you say yes I'll pull over to the side of the road and kiss you as you've never been kissed before."

"I don't know, Greg," she said doubtfully. "Shouldn't we wait a while? I've got that audition to get through first. Then I would have to establish myself at least somewhat in my career."

His eyes were on the smooth road ahead of them. A muscle twitched in his jaw.

"You were ready enough to marry Lyle," he said grimly.

"That was different. You know that, Greg."

After a long silence, he said gravely, "All right then.

Obviously it's up to you when, or even if, you want to marry me. But I don't think your refusal has anything to do with the audition or your career. And I promise you I'll keep asking until you say yes."

"You know, Greg," she said lightly, "you have the habit of treating me like someone who doesn't know her own mind."

"I don't think you do," he answered humorously, "but I love you just the same. Anyway, it's too nice a day to argue. It's also our last day for sightseeing in Brittany if we're leaving for the south of France tomorrow. So let me show you the Rance tidal-power plant. Okay?"

"Why don't we go to the Mont-Saint-Michel first? We can do the hydroelectric plant on the way back."

"Sometimes I think it's not hydroelectric power that binds us together," Greg said dryly.

Diane just looked out the window and smiled.

The hour's drive to Normandy and the "Marvel of the West," as the Mont-Saint-Michel was called, seemed short to Diane. She could have used more time to think about Greg's marriage proposal. She didn't understand why he hadn't accepted at face value her reason for refusing him at this time. Surely he could see that, having striven so hard for a musical career, she wouldn't give it up at a snap of his fingers. At the very least, he should have acknowledged her competence to know her own mind and to decide accordingly. She resented his lack of trust in her judgment about her own motives. His skepticism also left her with a feeling of uneasiness that she couldn't explain. Moreover, she wondered if it was wise to go to the Riviera with Greg. As heavenly as the trip sounded, would she be able to handle love and launching an operatic career at the same time?

"A penny for your thoughts," he said, glancing toward her with a wistful smile.

She didn't have the heart to spoil the day, their first together since finding out they were free to love, by telling him her fears and doubts. So she answered cheerfully, "I've been thinking that we're about to see one of the most spectacular sights in the world."

"I'm looking at the most spectacular sight in the world right now," he said, running his eyes from her hair, which tumbled in reddish-gold waves onto the collar of her crisp white suit, down to the soft outline of her breasts under her wood-violet silk shirt.

"Not as spectacular as that!" she answered reprovingly, pointing ahead of them.

Out of a vast expanse of shining wet sand rose a circular island of rock surmounted by a magnificent monastery, which was skirted by smaller granite buildings that rose in terraces on its flanks, and was topped by a slender spire. This was the famous Mont-Saint-Michel, where the first church was built in the eighth century, where the Benedictine monks built their abbey in the twelfth, and which was the only Norman fortress to withstand the assaults of the English forces during the Hundred Years War.

"Spectacular is the word, all right," Greg said. "You know, the Mont-Saint-Michel Bay has the highest tides in Europe. And the sea rushes in at over twenty miles an hour, the speed of a galloping horse."

"It's darn dangerous, too," Diane answered. "Now there's a causeway linking the rock with the mainland, but even so, fishermen are occasionally caught by the tides and drowned."

As Diane and Greg mounted the steep narrow street that led through the village of Saint-Michel, up to the abbey, Greg swept his arm toward the souvenir shops, restaurants, and small hotels that lined the street. "It's pretty touristy, isn't it?" he said with an air of faint disappointment.

"Not when you consider that it probably had the same aspect in the Middle Ages, except that then the shops sold devotional articles instead of postcards; the visitors were pilgrims, not tourists; and they were shown around by monks, not uniformed guides."

"You win, Teach," Greg said, laughing. "Only, to get

into the spirit of the thing, do you think we could skip the guided tour and just climb up on the ramparts—a knight and his lady, so to speak."

"You're willing to miss the cloister and the knights' hall and the dungeon?" Diane pouted a little.

"You've got it. Especially the dungeon."

"The village church has a gorgeous statue of Saint Michael slaying the dragon."

"Don't tempt me," he said dryly.

"Okay, the ramparts it is."

So they climbed hundreds of stairs cut in the granite cliffs until they reached the highest platform of the ancient fortifications and looked out at the miles of sand flats, beyond which lurked the sea.

"It's like being completely detached from earth, isn't it?" Diane mumured. "Like being suspended in time and space."

"I've had that feeling since I met you," Greg said. "The rest of the world seems to have fallen away, leaving just the two of us."

He took her in his arms and kissed her softly, letting his lips linger until, clasped to each other, they swayed and she felt what he had described, a falling away of the world around them. Then a far-off dull roar reached her ears. She tore herself from Greg's grasp and silently pointed seaward.

"My God," he breathed.

The sea was moving over the sand with incredible speed, engulfing it, ingesting it almost, it seemed to Diane. Greg put his arm around her, as though they were in danger from the advancing tide, which they weren't. Shortly, with the exception of the elevated dike where the cars and tour buses were parked, the Mont was completely surrounded by water.

"That's amazing," Greg said. "Talk about tidal power!" Glancing around, he said musingly, "It must be beautiful here at night." He put his hands on her waist and held her away from him. "What do you say?" he asked, looking tenderly into her eyes.

Wings of joy beat in her breast. All the tensions and

fears of the past weeks promised to give way before their new freedom to love. For an answer, she only nodded. But she knew he could tell by her eyes how much she wanted to spend the night with him. With his arm around her waist, he led her away from the rampart wall.

They chose a hotel with a view of the bay. Their room was as simple and austere as a monk's cell; still, there was an immediate appeal to Diane in the snowy bedspread and the fresh white curtains billowing at the open window like the clouds in the sky just beyond.

The hotel's restaurant was famous for its omelettes, cooked on an open fire in gleaming copper pans with long handles. Diane and Greg shared one, a smooth golden oval, tender and creamy inside, and accompanied it with a Pouilly-Fuissé, a light, dry white wine. Throwing convention to the winds, they followed the omelette with the local speciality — roast leg of lamb from flocks raised on the salt marshes around the Mont. Greg ordered a full-bodied red wine, a Saint-Emilion, with the lamb. Patriotically, they finished their meal with a Normandy Camembert and a glass of Calvados.

Afterward, they ascended the deserted street of the village. The tourists were gone, the shops were dark, and the parking lot was empty. Their footsteps rang against the cobblestones. As they climbed, the spire of the abbey, its flying buttresses, and its gargoyles stood out in sharp, dramatic relief against the moonlit sky. Below them, the narrow, winding street and the terraces and gardens were a confusing labyrinth whose geography was difficult to recall.

They stood again on the highest rampart and looked out across the sands, silver now in the moonlight instead of gold. The serenity of the night, the deep silence and peace of the place, permeated Diane's consciousness. They didn't speak, and she knew Greg felt the same way she did. This was to be their night, a night suspended in time and space, when only their love for each other would exist.

He put his hands on her shoulders and turned her toward

him, tilting her face up to him with one finger placed gently under her chin. "The moon has turned you to silver," he said tenderly. "Here and here and here." He touched her lightly on the face and lips and throat. Her senses responded with an echoing thrill that left her heart beating fast in anticipation.

Greg slid his fingers through her hair and brought her close to him. He bent his head and rested his lips on her cheekbone. "Moon goddess," he whispered, "I've waited a long time for you." He brushed his lips along her cheek until they met hers in a kiss that made Diane shiver with longing. Her soft lips clung to his, parting as his teeth tugged at the full lower curve. He found her tongue, and his own lingered on it. Then he drew it into his mouth, possessing it as she knew he would soon possess her.

When he lifted his lips from hers, he took her hand and together they wound their way down from the dark, silent ramparts to the hotel. Their simple room was showered with moonlight, and as they hungrily sought each other's mouths again its pale glow lit their entwined forms.

Greg kissed her passionately for a long time, then his mouth roamed down to her throat, creating islands of exquisite sensation on the way. His hands reached under her blouse and spilled restlessly over the planes of her back, ending with long strokes down her spinal column to the delicate little hollow at its base. Tremors of incandescent excitement ran up and down Diane's spine under Greg's masterful, caressing touch. The sweet agony continued as his mouth tugged gently at her ear lobe in fragile hints of a bite, while at the same time he dropped one hand to her rounded bottom, curving his sinewy fingers around the firm flesh.

With the other hand, he bent her gently back so his fervent lips could reach her swan-white throat again. Each hot, licking kiss left her throbbing with delight. And as his lips descended further, to the soft flesh that billowed out of the deep V of her blouse, a wave of desire ran through her veins like molten lava. The buttons of the blouse and her bra gave way under his deft hands. Reaching down, he took a coral nipple in his mouth and gently teased it with his strong white teeth before taking it into his eager mouth. As his tongue wove a magic web of ecstasy around the taut peak, she moaned softly at the passion uncurling within her.

"Diane! My own exquisite Diane," he whispered, dipping his face to the deep valley of her breasts. His lean, stubble-roughened cheek, virile and sharp against her soft flesh, sent fresh tremors of arousal through her, shock waves that rose to even further sensations of pleasure when he put his partly opened mouth on her breast and covered it with delectable wet kisses. All the while, the pressure of his manhood swelling against her promised the closer intimacy she so greatly desired.

As he took her lips with his again, it seemed to Diane that all the world lay in Greg's hands and the mouth that was warming hers, bringing it with slow, languid sweeps to fever pitch. Urgently, she pressed her lips against his, nibbling them gently with her small white teeth, then darting her tongue over each little love bite as though to heal that which needed no healing.

Slipping his hands once more inside her blouse, he cupped her breasts, pleasuring the soft globes with his fingers, while with gentle probes his tongue parted her lips. In smooth, gliding motions, he explored the moist sweetness of her mouth until, in a frenzy of longing, she caught his tongue with hers and caressed it in turn.

With their mouths still joined in a kiss, he lifted her up in his arms and carried her to the barely full-size bed.

"It's an awfully small bed," Diane observed.

"Just made for making love. And any maiden who refused was thrown into the quicksand."

Diane laughed. "What a horrible fate."

"It was a fate *worse* than a fate worse than death."

Flinging her arms out dramatically, Diane said, "Take me, I'm yours!"

As he removed her blouse and slid her skirt down over her hips, Greg grumbled playfully, "You could have worn something easier to take off, you know."

"Stop complaining. How did I know I was going to be seduced?"

Burying his face in her luxuriant hair, he murmured wickedly in her ear, "None of this would have happened if you had come to the Rance power plant with me."

Then he poised himself above her and spread her long hair so that it fanned out on the pillow like a swimmer's in water. "I like you that way, a golden-haired siren," he murmured, his brown eyes gleaming with mingled desire and amusement.

"You'll be shipwrecked," she warned playfully.

"The sooner the better," he breathed into her warm, waiting mouth as his tongue thrust deeply into the sweetness within. He bent his head and kissed the glossy skin of first her left, then her right shoulder. His lips traveled lower, to the smooth white slopes of her breasts. The eager spires of her nipples strained upward for his kiss, and when he took each pink bud in his mouth and tugged gently at it, Diane went taut with longing. Her long fingers slipped ferverishly under the waistband of his slacks, and in an instant he had eased himself out of them. The rest of his clothes quickly followed. Aflame with desire for the man she loved, Diane wrapped her arms around his waist and feathered her hands over his broad back and firm buttocks. She quieted with a slow caress the shudder that rose under her fingers and, with her lips, the groan that escaped him.

"God, how I want you, Diane. Say you want me too."

"I want you, Greg. I want you so."

He bent over her, and under his lips her belly felt soft and flat and hot. Diane reveled in the hands that held her so surely while his lips did such delicious things to her. His warm, moist breath on her skin was an aphrodisiac mist. She twisted sensuously under him, helping his large hands as they eased her lace-trimmed bikini panties over her hips and off her in one deft, delicate movement.

Diane wound her arms around his neck and brought him down on her. She put all her ardent love for him into a scorching kiss, and when she tore her lips away, it was to lie languid and supine as his mouth moved lingeringly from hers to each quivering nipple and across the smoothness of her belly to plant a kiss where she wanted it most.

Then his lips seized hers, passionately capturing her mouth. A quickening shaft of pleasure coursed through her, making her weak with longing. She felt his male hardness powerful against her waiting softness, then he parted her legs with his own. As he eased himself into her, she breathed a long sigh of contentment. "It's been so long, Greg, so very long."

"That part's over, Diane. This is a new life." His breath was warm against her ear, the very breath of life itself.

She pressed her fingers into the contours of his strong back as he surged against her like the magnificent tides that lay outside. Then he carried her up with him in an ever-rising spiral of unbearable joy. With all the strength that was in her, Diane held him close, meeting the driving rhythm that threatened to shatter her senses. Wave after sky-reaching wave of piercing ecstasy went through her. She had never known love like this—not even with Mike in the early days of their marriage.

"Diane, my goddess, my love!"

She knew from their mingled harsh breathing that they were approaching the summit. She tightened her hold as, hands on her hips, he lifted her against him. She shivered, her whole body straining toward release. A final thrust sent her over the edge, rocketing out into a luminous sky of blazing comets and stars like flaming candles.

For several minutes, they lay as they were, exhausted, their passion deliciously sated. They were too tired to say more than "I love you" before falling asleep in each other's arms. Sometime during the night, when the moon was down, Diane felt Greg's lips lazily nudging her nipples awake while his hand gently stroked the inside of her thigh. Her own hand responded with the same loving search, and she smiled in anticipation of the joy she would soon experience again. There would be days and nights of such rapture when they were on the Riviera. And afterward? For the briefest moment, before they again merged in love, Diane wondered which would be worse—to lose Greg by not marrying him or to marry him and lose him as she had Mike?

# - 10 -

THEY STARTED SOUTH on a blue and gold morning, their intention to bypass Paris and reach Avallon in northern Burgundy by late afternoon. Diane called ahead and reserved both a room and a table for dinner at an inn that was a favorite stopping place of Parisians bound for the Riviera.

She had put her cassette player on the front seat between them, and soon the music of Verdi's *Rigoletto* filled the car.

"Why don't you sing along with the tape?" Greg asked.

"I can't. It would strain my vocal cords."

"All right, then I will," and he launched into Rigoletto's famous song, "We are birds of a feather . . ."

"Greg!" Diane exclaimed. "You have a beautiful baritone voice. Have you ever taken lessons?"

Greg shook his head. "You should hear me sing in the shower." He glanced at her slyly. "That's an invitation."

When it was noon, to save time, they passed up the rest stops set in wooded groves and marked *Pique-Nique* in favor of one of the many "bridge restaurants" that spanned both directions of the *autoroute*. Besides a multipurpose store

**110**

that sold magazines, utility items, and local food special-
ities, there was a cafeteria where diners started down the
line with a hard roll plucked from a huge basket and finished
by selecting a bottle of wine or mineral water at the end.
In between were dishes that, even in cuisine-conscious
France, bore a remarkable resemblance to standard-fare cafeteria food.

Then they were rolling again through the beautiful countryside. Cornfields and wheel-shaped haystacks gave way
to the vineyards and cherry orchards of northern Burgundy.
The conical blue slate towers of a château crowned a distant
hill; the pointed spire of a church marked the approach to
a town. Sometimes the landscape was rougher. Granite out-
crops alternated with grassy fields, and dark rivers leapt
over smoothly rounded rocks between banks of overhanging
willows and rows of poplars.

Their room at the inn was charming, done in provincial
style with wallpaper of small lavender flowers and a print
bedspread and curtains.

Greg looked around him with a pleased smile. "How do
you like it?" he asked.

"It's very pretty," Diane said neutrally.

"Something wrong, goddess?"

She shook her head and smiled. "Let's eat. I'm starved.
And we have a dinner reservation, don't forget."

Diane hoped that a little wine and good food and the
relaxation of stopping after a long trip would dispel the
doubts that had occupied her mind all the way from Saint-
Cast. Greg's marriage proposal had put a hurdle in the path
of her headlong gallop toward happiness. She felt more and
more strongly that she couldn't even contemplate marriage
at this time. The audition for the opera company was looming up ahead of her, and it was absolutely essential that she
succeed. Without this success, Diane reasoned, she would
slip back into being the nonentity she was during her marriage to Mike. Without the clear-cut goal of a career, how
would she spend her days? Now that she had tasted the
pleasure of purposeful work, she couldn't give it up. Perhaps

she and Greg would be able to work something out later, but for the present she had to concentrate on getting her voice back and passing the audition.

Diane put these cares aside, however, as she dressed for dinner in a simple black cotton dress with white piping at the jewel neck and the waist, and four big white buttons on the elbow-length petal sleeves. In a wifely gesture, she straightened the collar of Greg's classic navy blazer before they walked down the stairs to the attractive dining room.

"Now I know why Burgundy is famous for its food," Greg said over the rim of the menu. He gave the voluminous red-covered *carte* a shake. "This thing's got more pages than *War and Peace*. What do you suggest?"

"How do you feel about snails?" Diane asked with a laugh. "They're a Burgundian speciality."

"I feel very strongly about snails," Greg said emphatically. "And my feeling is that their place is on the ground, not on my plate."

They finally decided on assorted hors d'oeuvres to start, trout from one of the many nearby rivers as the entrée, and a bottle of Chablis, which was one of the regional wines. They finished with blackberry sorbet and gingerbread dessert, a specialty of Dijon, the capital of Burgundy.

Dinner was a leisurely affair, given over to relaxation and a sensuous savoring of the excellent food. Diane and Greg were surrounded by other Riviera-bound couples in chic casual attire, lovers, most of them, holding hands across the table, gazing into each other's eyes, vivaciously exchanging dramatic items of news.

Looking around the room, Greg said, "This place is as pair oriented as Noah's ark." He raised Diane's hand to his lips, then held it in his. "I feel right at home, don't you?"

Diane laughed. "I think you're just glad I didn't order snails."

He shuddered. "It would have been the end of a perfect relationship." He added suspiciously, "You don't cook those things at home, do you?"

She shook her head, smiling.

"Good. I'm a steak and potatoes man, myself."

She ran her finger across his thumbnail, then gently pulled her hand away.

"What's the matter, Diane?" he asked quietly. "Is marriage a forbidden subject?" Her clear gray eyes clouded over with confusion. Quickly, jokingly, he added, "That's all right. It doesn't have to be steak and potatoes." He glanced around conspiratorially and lowered his voice. "I'd even eat snails . . . for you."

She laughed then and, holding out her spoon to him, said, "Try some of this blackberry sorbet instead." He took the spoon in his mouth and licked it clean, his eyes holding hers all the while in a smoldering glance. He fed her then with bites of his gingerbread. When Diane looked up, it was to the approving gaze of their fellow diners. These Americans knew how to behave, after all.

After dinner they mounted the stairs with their arms around each other's waists, and when the door closed behind them they fell into a greedy embrace. The slow build-up of their desire throughout dinner had reached fever pitch, and they devoured each other with their mouths. Holding her under the breasts with his strong hands, Greg raked Diane's lips and face with his kisses. His smooth tongue glided effortlessly into her avid mouth, to duel amorously with hers.

While she balanced herself on tiptoes, with her arms around his neck, in one deft stroke he zipped her dress open in back.

"Take it off," he whispered.

Eagerly, she slipped out of the dress and stood before him in a lacy black bra and black panties.

"So beautiful!" he murmured huskily, his brilliant dark eyes dreamy with desire.

He buried his face in the waves of scented golden hair that fell to her shoulders. "Love me tonight, Diane, as I love you."

Love him? Her senses were aflame with desire for him, and he held her heart in the palm of his hand. She had never

loved Mike or any other man as she loved Greg Kimball.
She unbuttoned his shirt, slipped it off, and laid her hand
on his warm skin, curling her fingers in the dark mat of hair
on his chest, then rubbing the back of her hand across his
nipples. Feeling them peak, she bent her head and kissed
each in turn, relishing the pleasure she knew he was gar-
nering. Her long, nimble fingers undid his belt. Slipping
her hands inside his pants, she slid them down over his
narrow hips.

As he swung her up into his arms and carried her to the
bed, she ran her hands over his bare torso and laughed
joyously.

"Moon goddess," he whispered as he laid her down between the cool sheets.

Laughing impishly up at him, she said, "There's no
moon."

He paused in the act of easing off her panties, his hands
on her satiny thighs. "Do you want to be worshiped or not?"

Laughing, she moved sinuously under his touch and said,
"Yes, worship me."

He removed the wisp of black lace that covered her
breasts and trailed his lips langorously down their creamy
slopes. Cuddled between his big hands, Diane gave herself
over to the joy of feeling each nipple licked into an erect
little flame by his tongue. Her body yearned for him. She
wanted to feel all of him against her own demanding flesh.
She moaned and arched upward toward him. He dropped
his mouth to the inward tuck of her navel, kissing it with
moist, parted lips. Then he trailed his kisses downward
across the smooth flatness of her belly to the nest of golden
curls between her thighs.

Panting now, almost delirious with desire, she ran her
hands over his smooth back, narrow hips, and hard buttocks,
straining as close to him as she could.

"Now, darling! Make it now," she breathed.

Then they were going up the roller coaster again, up and
up until with a soft cry she reached the top and, hearing his

answering cry, began the downward descent.

Afterward, they lay entwined like one being with more arms and legs, Diane thought dreamily, than even two people should have.

"I want you, Diane. Not just for a month or two, but for the rest of our lives. Why won't you say you'll marry me?"

She didn't answer. She couldn't. Her love for Greg and marrying him were two different things. All she could do was put her arms around his bare body and whisper "I love you." They made love again then and once more as dawn was breaking.

Waking up with the morning and freeing herself from Greg's arms, Diane sat up and said with a pout, "I bought a sexy new nightgown for this trip, and I haven't even worn it."

"You didn't need it," he pointed out logically.

"Never mind, I'm wearing it tonight."

She jumped out of bed just as a knock on the door sounded.

"Who's that?" Greg asked, pulling the sheet up over his naked form.

"The chambermaid. I ordered an early breakfast." Diane grinned wickedly from the threshold of the bathroom. "Just call out '*Entrez!*'" she said airily, and disappeared.

They continued south, past the great name-bearing vineyards of Burgundy and the medieval cities whose church steeples punctuated the sky and whose rooftops were curiously checkerboarded in colored tiles. They rode in renewed intimacy, sitting close, Diane's hand on Greg's thigh. And when they entered the long tunnel that ran through the metropolis of Lyons, Greg took one hand from the wheel and put it around her waist.

"This is the longest road tunnel in France," Diane said.

"What do you say we just ride back and forth in it?"

"I've got a better idea. Lyons is famous for its sausage. Why don't we stop and get some, and have a picnic today?"

"Sometimes I think the only reason you love me is because I feed you."

"You guessed it," she said cheerfully.

Shopping with Greg became an adventure as they selected a tasty garlicky sausage, a loaf of crusty bread, and the well-known Lyonnais cheese, Mont d'Or. Marriage to a man who brought such gusto to the most mundane activities would certainly make for an exciting life, Diane thought wistfully before sternly reminding herself she mustn't think this way. She must focus on the upcoming audition, on the launching of her operatic career. And she must remember that the more endearing Greg was, the more it would hurt when he tired of monogamy and began to stray. She wouldn't go through that again, not ever, and especially not with Greg.

Because they were driving, Diane insisted that they buy a large bottle of mineral water instead of wine, and they started off again into a different landscape. Here, to protect the vineyards, were rows of wind-bent dark-green pines and cypresses rather than poplars, and the farmhouses were built of old stone topped by flat red-tiled roofs. This was Provence, whose sunniness and luminous skies had made it a country of painters. Some, like Cézanne, were native sons; others—Van Gogh, Renoir, Matisse, and Picasso—strangers from other parts.

They picnicked along the bank of a stream where the grass was starred with white and yellow wild daisies. Greg cut the sausage and bread with a knife he had bought, and they took turns drinking from the bottle of Evian. They threw the pieces of bread that were left into the river and watched a V-shaped formation of mallards break ranks for them. Then they lay down side by side in the thick grass and stared up into the leaves of a plane tree.

"What are you thinking of?" Greg turned over on his stomach and put his hand on the underside of her breast, tautened by the upward stretch of her arms cushioning her head.

"That I'd like this moment to never end." She laughed

wistfully. "I'm ready to take up your suggestion of riding that tunnel in Lyons back and forth."

"Do you dread the audition that much?" he asked, surprised.

"No. Yes," she added quickly. It was easier to talk about the audition than marriage. And it was true, she did dread the audition.

"Are you afraid you won't pass it?" His face was concerned, and Diane was touched by his empathy.

"It's pretty iffy at this point," she admitted frankly. "My throat has improved since we left Brittany, but I still don't know whether my voice has returned."

He grimaced. "I'd hate to think that my insistence that we climb those cliffs might have ruined your chance at the career you want."

"Even if we hadn't done that, my vocal quality and technique might not have been good enough. Madame Daudon certainly didn't think they were," she added with a rueful laugh.

"You're a good sport, Diane."

Propping herself up on her elbows, she threw her head back and laughed. "Don't you know that's the worst thing you can call a woman?"

He placed his finger carefully on her upwardly arching throat. "Okay, then you're piebald, like a horse."

Still laughing, she said, "Thanks a lot."

"No, really. The sunlight through those leaves is dappling you black and white." He leaned over her. "Where would you rather be kissed—on the sunny patches or the shadows?" Illustrating, he made irregular patterns with his fingers on her face and neck and her shoulders, bare now since she had removed the jacket put on against the chill of the morning.

A sudden fear struck Diane. If they made love now, would he ask her to marry him again? And then what would she say? So as he lowered his lips to her cheek, to kiss a section that lay in either sun or shadow, she didn't know which, she turned her head abruptly and jumped up.

"We'd better start or we won't make Nice tonight," she said.

Greg stood up, too. He thrust his hands in his pockets and tilted backward on his heels. "That's nonsense," he drawled, "and you know it. What's wrong, Diane?"

She raised her chin and looked off into the distance, at the lavender hills terraced with vineyards. At a loss for words, she tried to joke. "I didn't bring my sexy nightgown."

"Really! I thought it was packed somewhere between the sausage and the cheese." In one long step, he was in front of her. His hands on her shoulders, he looked deep into her eyes. "Is that all you think I want of you? How can you, when I've told you so often I want us to marry." His tenderness turned steely. "I didn't take you away from Lyle just to have an affair with you."

She became angry then. Even a man as big-natured as Greg could turn macho when the chips were down. "You didn't *take* me away from Lyle," she retorted. "Neither you nor any other man could do that. Lyle and I both saw we weren't meant for each other, that's all."

"And who were you meant for, goddess?" he asked slyly, his admiring eyes on her brilliant hair and flushed countenance.

"Not you!" she snapped. "Not anybody. I was *meant* for myself." She started to pick up the remains of the picnic. Tears of frustration welled up in her gray eyes. She had been crazy to let herself be detoured by love. All men were the same. Sooner or later, they showed their true stripes.

When he put his hands on her bare shoulders, she tried to shake them off. But he slid his fingers under the spaghetti straps of her sun dress and held her in a gentle but firm grasp.

"You're terrific when you get angry like that. You don't mind a stormy marriage, do you? Just so I can look at you when you flare up." The narrow straps were off her shoulders now, and his hand was cuddling the convex mounding of her breast. "I just want to make an honest woman of you," he whispered seductively, bending his face to hers. Abruptly, he stepped back. "You smell of garlic," he said, surprised.

"It's the sausage, you idiot. So do you—smell of garlic."

Sniffing deeply, he said, "Actually, I like garlic."

Diane laughed. "So do I."

He looked down at her with a sly smile. "I guess we're stuck with each other now."

How could she resist him? she thought, as he bent his head to her. She loved his silliness, his sensitivity, the fact that they always had something to say to each other. And as his mouth seized hers and her lips opened flowerlike under his, she thought again: How can I resist him when he makes me feel ripe and womanly and honey-sweet, as no other man ever has?

Gently, he lowered her onto the blanket they had spread for their picnic. Poised above her, his eyes caressing her face, he said, "I want you like this. In the sunlight, under a tree, with the smell of earth around us." Suddenly, his mood changed. His eyes grew hot and his voice rasped in his throat. "I want you . . . any way I can get you, Diane."

This was a new Greg, a man she hadn't known before. His lips burned hers with hard, demanding kisses. His tongue triumphantly took possession of her mouth's rich velvet. Urgently, his hands slipped the sun dress down to her waist. Lifting her full breasts from her bra, he filled his hands with the sun-dappled mounds.

"Beautiful," he breathed. "So beautiful."

Gently then, he passed the sensitive underside of his wrist over one rosy peak until it hardened and pressed against his skin.

"You look like a dryad," he said. "A tree nymph."

Diane laughed. "I thought I was supposed to be a temptress."

"That too. Can you imagine how you'd feel after you had been shut up in a tree for a million years?"

She wound her arms around his neck and pulled him down on her. The sign of his arousal pressed her thigh like a steel rod. His eyes were ardent, his breathing harsh. "The way I feel now," she whispered.

"Not so fast. I may hold out for a wedding ring. Will you marry me, Diane?"

"I love you. Isn't that enough?"

A long shudder rocked his big frame. Slowly, deliberately, he raised himself from above her and stood up. He walked to the lazy dark stream and, picking up a stone, flung it onto the water, making it skip before it sank in a circle of ever-widening ripples. He did this with another stone, and another. She stood also and watched him as she arranged her dress. His neck was stiff, his shoulders bulged with the tension in his muscles as he strove for self-control. She, too, was making a supreme effort to quiet her racing heart and quell the torrent of unsatisfied need that flooded through her.

Finally, he turned and faced her. "What kind of love is it, Diane, that avoids commitment? I've told you before and I'll tell you again—I want to spend the rest of my life with you. I want us to have children together. I don't want any other woman, and I don't want you to have any other man. I want you to be my wife."

Diane shook her head. "You just want a wife."

"And what do you want? A good time? Something to give your voice fire and emotion? Or maybe to relax you after a hard day at the opera?"

His tone was hard and contemptuous. Diane had no answer for him. No one, not even he, would believe it if she said she loved him too much to marry him. She knew now that she wouldn't be able to stand it if he ran out on her physically or emotionally. She had borne up under Mike's philandering, and she could have tolerated Lyle's. But it would tear her apart, literally destroy her, if Greg did that to her.

So she didn't answer him, but instead turned to go back to the car. In the silence of the shaded dell, she heard his muttered "All right, Diane, I won't bother you anymore." And she kept going, opening the car door, settling herself in the front seat, and not looking at him when he threw the blanket in and eased his big frame behind the steering wheel.

They rode like that, in silence, for miles. When they started talking again, it was not with the relief and the laughs of lovers making up after a quarrel, nor did they return to the easy intimacy and companionship of before. They were polite and careful this time. And Diane's heart seemed to die within her at each stilted observation she made about the countryside they were passing through and Greg's quick agreement.

She longed to say "Yes, I will marry you." She even daydreamed a little about his stopping the car after she had said it and taking her in his arms. She fantasized his firm mouth pushing hers into new soft shapes and his strong sensitive hands caressing her. But she remained silent. She had said, "Yes, I will marry you" to Mike and had almost ruined her life. She wouldn't say yes again until she had a career to fall back on, to bury the inevitable heartbreak in.

# - *11* -

NICE, WITH ITS traffic-choked streets and strident auto horns, was a shock after the quiet of the countryside. Diane vaguely remembered the city from a visit she'd made there with her aunt as a teenager. She searched the streets eagerly now to reacquaint herself with their geography.

"There's a good little hotel not far from where we are now," she said. "If you'd be so kind as to drop me there . . ."

"Don't be ridiculous," Greg said brusquely. "There must be all of seventeen rooms in the villa I've gotten for us; you won't have to see me at all, since that seems to be your object." Paying no attention to her protest, he made a left turn, saying, "It's up here, in the hills above the city."

They wound their way up to the highest of the three parallel roads cut into the mountains that loomed above the Mediterranean. This was the Grande Corniche, the road built by Napoleon on the site of an old Roman road. Looking down, Diane could see Nice sprawled out below them beside the tranquil blue water of the Bay of Angels.

Then a villa, white as a wedding cake, with classical columns and a stand of starkly green cypresses, caught her eye. It stood alone on a promontory with a sheer drop below.

"How do you think they get their bread in the morning?" Diane asked lazily, making conversation.

Greg took his eyes off the narrow twisting road long enough to flash a grin at her. "You'll find out soon enough. That's our villa."

Diane swallowed hard. "But it's miles from anywhere!"

"Not really. There's a village hidden by those trees over there." Greg pointed to a small forest of fir and birch.

"But how will I get to Nice? I'll have to practice with a vocal coach, and I may have to see a doctor, and I'll certainly have to go there for the audition."

"No problem. There's a chauffeur in the village who'll come in a minute when we call. I've also hired a household staff to come and go as we please."

"You've thought of everything."

"There was a time when I hoped this would be our honeymoon cottage." He said this with wry humor as he steered the Renault up the sweeping circular drive.

The idea of this imposing modern château being called a cottage made Diane smile.

"You didn't rent this from Holiday Homes," she said.

"All they had available were garrets in the old part of Nice."

He was joking, of course, but as they alighted in front of more Doric columns than the Parthenon boasted, Diane wished that they *were* in one of those sunny old-fashioned apartments with the metal shutters thrown open, a canary on the windowsill, a neighbor's blue working clothes drying on a balcony, and the garlic-heavy aroma of good cooking everywhere. She didn't want to get away from him in a seventeen-room mausoleum. She wanted to be in a place where every time she turned around, she brushed against him, and where the bedroom was only a border for the big four-poster set in the very center, as befitted its importance.

Instead, she found herself being ushered down a long hallway by a correctly attired maid to a suite double the size of any apartment in old Nice and with a view of a flower-blanketed hillside rather than a wooden box of geraniums on an iron balcony. Throwing open the windows immediately, Diane breathed in the scent of lavender and thyme and caught a glimpse of the sea far below. Granted, the view was spectacular and the rooms tastefully decorated, but the silence once the maid had left was oppressive, and Diane didn't know how to occupy the hours until dinner.

Greg had told her that there was a music room in the villa and that this was one reason he had chosen the house over others. Diane's throat felt so much better that she dared to hope she was completely cured. But there was only one way to tell, and she decided to go to the music room and try her voice.

The maid had hung up her clothes and, after showering, Diane slipped into a loose-fitting cotton djellaba bordered along the low-cut neck and the flowing sleeves with flower-embroidered lace. Its brilliant red, rather than paling her hair, brought out its copper highlights, and the garment promised to be cool and comfortable for the work she hoped to be doing at the piano.

As she wandered through the rooms of the house, she began to change her first impressions of it and to like it. The architect had obviously used passive solar techniques in planning the building, as it was airy and cool, yet every room was awash with natural light. The furnishings were contemporary but comfortable, and there were a number of good modern paintings that, in typical Riviera style, enlivened the white walls with bright splashes of color.

The music room was particularly attractive. French doors opened onto a garden with a fountain, and the soft plashing of the water formed a counterpoint to Diane's first tentative scales. The silence of the house was a boon, and she sensed for almost the first time how much noise there was in daily life and how difficult it was to sing against it.

As Diane continued singing, she realized, first with apprehension that it might not be true but then with increasing confidence, that her voice had indeed returned. Her relief was so great that she had to get up from the piano and go to the window to contain her emotion.

She heard Greg enter behind her and turned around. She stood still a moment, her head and shoulders thrown proudly back. When she saw the slow, deliberate ripple of his brilliant dark eyes across her breasts and thighs, where, despite its loose fit, the garment clung, her heart responded with a soft hammer-beat of joy. His anger hadn't driven out his love for her.

"My voice has come back," she said joyously. "I won't even have to go to a doctor." She waved her arms widely, and the sleeves of the djellaba fluttered like butterfly wings. "I'll just stay here and practice."

"You like it then—the villa, I mean. At first I thought you didn't."

"You were right. It looked like Grand Central Station without the trains. But now I think it's beautiful." She gestured toward the piano. "Thank you for renting this particular villa for me—for us, rather," she added, looking full at him.

"I sent the staff away," he said, taking a step toward her. Catching her look of alarm, he added with a laugh, "There's a microwave and plenty of cooked food."

Diane laughed, too. "It's hardly a place where one can run out for a hamburger, is it?"

He ran his hands up inside the flowing embroidered sleeves, making her smooth flesh tingle. "Shall we call it a lovers' quarrel, darling?" he asked, searching her eyes for her answer.

It had been more than that, and he knew it as well as she. But they couldn't stay away from each other, no matter what the cost. So with her gray eyes softly gleaming, she nodded.

"Where's that sexy nightgown you brought along?"

"The maid put it on my bed."

"That's what I like, well-trained help. Well, where will it be, your place or mine?"

"I haven't seen your room yet."

"Then I'll meet you there."

"How will I find it?" she wailed.

"I've made a trail of rose petals." He looked so boyishly pleased with himself that Diane had to laugh. "I don't believe it!" she said.

"Seeing is believing!" With that he lifted her in his arms and carried her up the wide staircase. Then he set her down in a field of soft pink petals that stretched from her door to another white one farther down the hall. He gave her a little slap on the bottom that lingered and became a caress. "Hurry up and put on that nightgown before I show you what a real bed of roses feels like."

"You were pretty sure of yourself," Diane said slyly.

"Let's just say 'hoping,'" he answered softly.

A few minutes later, Diane was half slipping, half walking in rose petals up to her ankles. The unfamiliar sensation of gossamer-softness on her bare feet delighted her. She kicked the petals up around her, then tried skipping among them. She shook her head in admiration. Only Greg would have thought of a trail of rose petals. Their source was obvious; the rose bushes in the garden were loaded with blooms. And Diane supposed he had asked the maid to strew the carpet with them while she was practicing. They were velvety under her feet, until a sharp sting of pain told her that she had stepped on a thorn. A trickle of blood stained the pink flowers. Diane examined her foot. The thorn was gone. She stuck a few petals over the deep scratch and thought nothing more about it until she entered Greg's room.

Then, looking down at her feet, she was horrified to see a dime-sized red stain on the thick white carpet.

"I'm bleeding on your rug!" she wailed.

In one quick move, Greg picked her up and carried her to the marble sink in the connecting bathroom. He turned on the gold seahorse-shaped faucets and gently laved her foot in warm, soapy water. He patted it dry with a towel thicker than Tante Yvonne's rugs and kissed the red pinprick that remained. Then, lifting the champagne-colored chiffon of her nightgown, he kissed her with exquisite slowness from the instep of her arched foot to the top of her smooth, supple thigh. The pleasure he gave her was heightened by the sight of the springy dark hair on his chest as his brown velour robe fell partly open. She longed to curl her fingers in the furry mat, but now was not the time. Instead, she put her arms around his neck and whispered in his ear, "The marble is cold—you know where."

Laughing, he scooped her up in his arms again. "This is what comes from being rich—roses and thorns and marble baths."

*"And* a stained carpet," she reminded him as he carried her into the bedroom. "It's too late to wash the stain out. You'll have to have the carpet cleaned or recompense the owner of the villa," she said sternly.

"Yes, my Holiday Homes troubleshooter, I think the owner of the villa should be recompensed." He bent his head and kissed her, raising her at the same time so that he could press his lips more firmly against hers. His strong arms ensnared her, bringing her closer to the magic of his sexy male flesh, and Diane was pierced with the aching need to be joined to him again. Playfully, she reached her bare foot inside his robe and opened it completely.

"You did that to *me* once. Remember?" she said mischievously.

He grinned. "Okay, we're even, but the next move is mine." He laid her on the bed and, balancing himself above her, showered her face and neck with moist kisses that melted like snowflakes on her heated skin. With one quick movement, he divested himself of his robe. Then he plunged his hands under the flower-appliquéd lace that covered her breasts and peeled the frothy gown off her, leaving her body a rosy pink and gold in the sunshine that filled the room.

"I don't think you care much for nightgowns," she said.

"I never wear them," he growled.

Her eyes laughed up into his as their lips joined in a long, voluptuous kiss. "Let me love you," he murmured, and his hands touched her reverently everywhere in caresses that were acts of love. His lips followed, sometimes in light, fleeting motions down her arms or sensuous little tugs at her nipples or hot, darting strokes of his tongue in her navel. He planted a border of kisses along the inside of her thigh, then his lips reached the velvety petals of her desire. Diane felt a warm melting at the very core of her being. Every atom in her body seemed to be pulsing with a need for completion.

"Oh, Greg, please," she whispered. "Please, now. I love you so."

"I love *you*, Diane," he answered huskily as he entered her slowly and lovingly.

Then words were drowned in a dialogue of gasps and sighs. Their hearts drummed together. Their breath was a single warm stream. Diane gave herself completely to the overwhelming ecstasy, to the throbbing, shimmering joy they shared in the final crescendo.

A long moment afterward, Diane lifted drowsy lashes to Greg's dark eyes, gold-flecked from the sun, gazing lovingly down at her. He still lay on top of her; their bodies, wet with perspiration, were intimately entwined. Diane turned her head. The nightgown she had spent so much time selecting was a pale frothy heap on the white rug. Her eyes traveled farther to the small red stain. What had Greg said about the villa's owner?

"Who owns this villa?" she asked.

"The man who's kissing you now." He had gotten up on his knees and was covering her face and neck and shoulders with kisses. Laughing, she pushed him away.

"No, seriously, Greg," she insisted.

"You didn't like that answer?" His eyes were wide with mock surprise. "How about the man who's doing this . . . and this . . . ?"

He was tickling her now, in excitingly intimate places. She turned on her stomach to protect herself; then, remembering her question, turned around again and faced him.

"Well, Greg, do you?"

"Do I love you?" He shrugged elaborately and stuck his lower lip out. "I don't know. You're nice to sleep with, but I don't think you're the kind of woman I'd want to marry."

"Greg!" she screamed at him, in total frustration. She reached for a pillow and hurled it at his head.

Laughing, he caught it and said, "Okay, I confess. I bought the joint. I figured it for our home when we're husband and wife and you're singing with the Riviera opera company."

Her gray eyes grew serious then. "That was a crazy thing to do, Greg. I may not pass the audition, and I haven't said I'd marry you."

"Suppose you passed. Would you marry me then? We could always make some kind of living arrangements while you were singing in an opera."

"Do we have to discuss it now?"

"I think we do," he said firmly. "Women no longer choose between marriage and a career, even a career in opera. They can have both, and God knows I'm willing to make any accommodation you want. So what really gives, Diane? Why won't you marry me?"

She lay for a long time without answering. Finally, in a small voice, she said, "Would it sound crazy if I said I don't want to marry you because I love you?"

He settled himself beside her, and with his arms curved around her he said softly, "No, it wouldn't. Why don't you tell me, Diane."

She took a deep breath, then started slowly. "I've heard women say things like 'When I found out my husband cheated on me, I just threw the cad out and found somebody else,' but it wasn't like that with me. I had really given my life to Mike—totally. I wore the clothes he liked, waited for him to come home at night, made his friends my friends even though I didn't have much in common with them, and wasted my musical education on silly little volunteer jobs for a suburban operetta company because he didn't want me to work. I thought..." Her voice caught in her throat then and she couldn't go on.

"That if you tried harder than your mother, you would succeed in keeping your man?" he asked gently, stroking her hair.

"I guess that's it. And I thought I had succeeded. I never dreamed that Mike would be unfaithful. And when I found out, I went to pieces for a while. Then I thought that it was somehow my fault, so I tried even harder to please him. But at the same time, even though I knew I shouldn't, I also started watching for signs of infidelity. And I found out about another time, and yet another.

"I confronted him with what I had discovered. He assured me that he loved me and explained that these were just physical affairs, which I was foolish to take seriously, particularly since there wasn't anything I could do about it. Men simply required more variety than women. I knew I couldn't live with that kind of a relationship, not with a man I had once loved as passionately as I loved Mike. Although I didn't tell him, I started thinking about divorce. Then he got sick, and I wouldn't leave him."

Greg's hand lingered on her hair in long, comforting strokes. "You can trust *me*, Diane. I would *never* be unfaithful to you."

How can I know that, Greg? she wanted to whisper. How will I ever really know?

## - *12* -

"I FEEL LIKE Violetta in the second act of *La Traviata*,"
Diane said with a laugh. She and Greg were in the garden
of the villa, breakfasting at a wrought-iron table covered
with a cloth in a gay Provençal print. Around them were
hills still tied with ribbons of fog; and below, a toy boat, a
cruise ship pinned to the smooth blue water of the bay. The
morning air was fresh and tartly sweet with a mélange of
scents from the herb-covered hills and the flowers and citrus
trees in the garden.

"You mean the heroine who dies of consumption?" Greg
glanced with exaggerated disbelief at Diane's buxom figure
and then at the basket of flaky brown croissants on the table,
the silver dish of country butter, and the small pot of local
honey.

Laughing again, Diane drew her flowered peignoir around
her. "Don't be mean. Besides, Violetta doesn't die until the
end of the opera. At the beginning of the second act, she's
happier than she has ever been in her life, living in a country
house like this with Alfredo."

Greg leaned forward. "Are you happier than you have ever been in your life, Diane?"

"Yes," she said simply.

"Then why don't we make it for a lifetime? I don't want any other woman but you, and I never will."

"'Never' is a long time, Greg." She bent her head to her coffee cup. She didn't dare look at him. She loved him so much; every part of him was so dear to her—his well-shaped head, the heavy line of his jaw, his firm mouth that had teased her and loved her all over and brought her to the height of rapture night after night here in the villa—that she was afraid if she looked at him she would say yes, she would marry him.

"All right, so 'never' is a long time," he said brusquely. "What if the marriage lasted only five years or even only one? At least we would have made a commitment, given testimony of our love. Remember I told you once that you have to give to get? Well, I've got news for you, Diane. Life is risky. *Love* is risky. It's an adventure, damn it, not a security blanket."

He got up and pushed his chair back. Then he flung his linen napkin on the table and strode away. Diane heard the French doors bang shut behind him. She remained sitting at the table, loath to enter the house and meet Greg while he was so angry. At least, she thought wryly, he got high marks for honesty. He had practically admitted that sooner or later he would tire of marriage. It might take five years or only one. But it was bound to happen; that's the way men were.

She finally got up and went into the music room. Absently, she ran her hands over the keys. If nothing else, she always had music, she reflected. Perhaps Greg was partially right, maybe music was her means of escape into a structured world, one that she could control. But she didn't care. It was her joy, her solace. And if she passed the audition, it would be her livelihood.

She was practicing every morning now with a vocal coach whom Greg's hired chauffeur picked up and and returned to Nice. Denise Michard was an older woman who seemed to know everyone in the musical circles of the Riviera. Moreover, she had a soothing personality and was much easier to work with than the abrasive Madame Daudon had been.

With time to kill before Madame Michard arrived, Diane started to play the love duet that the sorceress-princess Esclarmonde and the French knight Roland sing on the enchanted isle to which Esclarmonde has Roland brought through her magic. Diane had played the tape of the opera over and over, so that not only she but Greg too knew it by heart. They even joked about the villa's being their enchanted island.

As she played, Diane suddenly felt Greg's hands on her shoulders, smoothing themselves against the chiffon of her peignoir. He started singing Roland's part, hamming it up with exaggerated gestures and diction. Diane knew that this was his way of making up and sang the duet with him, assuring him, in Esclarmonde's words, that although he couldn't see her because she had to remain veiled, she was *belle et désirable*.

Dropping out of character, Greg breathed, "And so you are, Diane, beautiful and desirable." He ran his hands down her sides and over her breasts, pulling her against him as he stood behind her. A feeling of sadness swept over Diane. Mike had loved her in that way, too. He often told her how beautiful she was, and he certainly had desired her night after night—for a while, anyway. The thought made her stiffen in Greg's embrace. He put his hands under her chin and tilted her face upward. Looking down at her, he said quietly, "What is it, Diane?"

"I don't want to be beautiful and desirable. I want to be homely and sit by the fire with a homely husband and make three wishes."

Greg laughed. "And one of those wishes would be to be beautiful. The second would be to have a handsome husband. And the third . . ."

"Would be to have him faithful to me," Diane finished.

"And you think he would be more apt to be faithful if you weren't beautiful?" Greg asked, surprised.

"Of course. Beauty is superficial. It attracts superficial people. It fades. The grass is always greener in another pasture. There's always somebody more beautiful to be won."

"I get it. You don't want to be Cinderella; you want to be one of the stepsisters."

"I don't even want the frog prince," Diane said ruefully. "I want the frog."

"Hey, watch it. You're getting too close to home, there."

He moved around to the front of the piano and, hands resting on the baby grand, stood looking at her.

"I wonder if it's really men you distrust, Diane."

"What do you mean?" As always, when he looked at her in that searching way he had, she felt her heart flutter with anxiety.

"Maybe it's yourself you don't have confidence in. Maybe you think because you lost one man, you can't hold on to any man."

She got up and faced him. "I think you've been spending too much time with headhunters and drum speakers, Greg. Women no longer 'lose' men or 'hold' them as though they were possessions. Not only do I *not* distrust myself, I have more faith in myself than ever. I've smartened up. I'll never get burned again, believe me." She glanced at her watch. "I have to change. Denise will be here soon."

Nevertheless, for the rest of the day, Diane thought about what Greg had said. Was it true? Was self-distrust her inheritance—Mike's legacy and that of her bitter, quarreling parents? Without reaching a conclusion, she put the idea aside. Of necessity, the audition had to occupy all her emotional energies at this time.

The dents Madame Daudon had made in her confidence had been gradually smoothed out by Denise Michard's praise. But, at the same time, as what she called A-day approached, Diane became increasingly nervous. Moreover, the constant veering between self-assurance and uncertainty was beginning to wear her down. And it didn't help that the Riviera was in the midst of a heat wave. Pleasantly languorous days and balmy nights had given way to scorching heat and forest fires. Even the villa on top of the hill was warm at night, so that one evening when Greg suggested dinner and a ride along the coastal road, the Corniche Inférieure, Diane gladly agreed.

They went to a hole-in-the-wall restaurant unknown to tourists and ate a local fish, *loup de mer*, cooked at the table over a little fire of fennel twigs doused with brandy. They lingered over dinner, and it was late when they left the restaurant.

"Where would you like to go?" Greg asked, helping Diane into the Renault.

"No place in particular. Why don't we just drive until we find a good place to walk on the beach?"

"How about your throat?"

"In this weather? It's more apt to dry out than become sore."

Traffic was light at that hour, and except for a few cafés, the little towns they passed through were dark. Greg stopped the car at a cove where a stretch of deserted beach glistened white against the black water. They got out of the car and stood hand in hand for a moment, listening to the murmurous ebb and flow of the Mediterranean.

"You'd think there'd be lovers here," Diane said, looking around at the empty sand.

"There are." He drew her to him and drank endlessly of her lips, sending one deep, all-pervasive thrill coursing through her.

After he had freed her and they started walking, Diane said, "This looks like a good beach. We'll have to come back some day with our suits."

"We don't need them now," he whispered suggestively, taking her in his arms again.

"Greg! I really think you should do something about this compulsion you have to swim in the nude on French beaches."

"Maybe I'll write a travel book, *Skinny-Dipping in Europe, or How To Pack Light."*

"Swimsuits don't take up much room, silly."

"These do." Holding her with one hand, he quickly unzipped her cotton frock with the other. He was starting to unhook her bra when she stopped him. "Let's go swimming," he coaxed. "It's warm enough."

"Oh, no! You're not making a skinny-dipper out of me."

He ran his hands over her full breasts and gave the curved cheeks of her derriere a little swat. "Skinny? Never! Thank God."

Pushing him away, she zipped her dress closed again. "You go for a swim if you like. I can't take the chance because of my throat."

"All right," he said, unbuttoning his shirt. "But you'll never know what you're missing."

"I've gone for midnight swims before."

"Ah, but I was planning to make love to you."

"In the water?" she asked, surprised and intrigued.

"Why not? We, that is to say life, began in the sea."

"I know," she replied ironically. "But we've been on land a long time. Besides, with my audition so close..."

"So? I've heard tenors always make love the night before they sing."

"I'm not a tenor, Greg," she reminded him. "I'm a soprano."

"Then it would be all right. Sopranos do it on the high seas."

She groaned at his joke, and he flashed an appreciative grin as, completely undressed now, he sprinted toward the dark water.

Diane paced the sand for a while, breathing deeply of the warm, barely salty air, so different from the sharp tang of the Brittany coast. Then she glanced toward the water, worried because Greg hadn't returned. Had he gone in too soon after dinner? Was he suffering a cramp out there alone, unable even to call her? She went to the sand's edge and peered anxiously out over the black void. There was no sign of him.

She screamed his name, her voice shrill with fear. The

surface of the water broke then, not far from where she was standing. He came striding toward her, boldly male, as he had looked the first time she saw him.

"Greg! I was so worried."

"Glad to hear it, goddess." His big arms swooped her in close to him, and wet as he was, she permitted his embrace. Nothing but the solid feel of him—his wet, slick skin and dripping hair—could soothe her. More acutely than ever, Diane realized how much she loved him. Once I've passed the audition, she vowed silently, we'll go to the wedding chapel in Menton. She reached up and kissed him sweetly on the lips; he didn't know it, but it was a promise. Then she gently pushed him away before she got too wet.

When A-day came, she refused Greg's offer to drive her into Nice because she wanted the distraction of driving herself. To quell her mounting nervousness, she tried to keep the day as normal as possible. She sang a few scales in the morning to confirm that her voice was "there." She had no more than a cup of broth for lunch so that her breathing wouldn't be restricted by a full stomach. Then, taking both the vocal score of Esclarmonde's song and another aria in case she was asked to sing an encore, Diane waved a jaunty good-bye to Greg and started out.

On the way to Nice, to bolster her courage, Diane mentally compiled a list of her assets. Her musicianship was sound. She had some stage experience to her credit, albeit only in the small, local Forestville Operetta Company. Her teachers and vocal coaches had assured her that both her voice and her technique, although not problem-free, were very good. And she had the three foreign languages that most opera companies required. Her French was fluent, her Italian excellent, and her German satisfactory, if a bit shaky. Moreover, she had specialized in the French repertoire and had selected an aria from the seldom-performed *Esclarmonde* in order to show her versatility and because it was a good vehicle for her coloratura soprano voice.

Diane's self-enforced calm lasted until she reached the theater, where, clutching her music backstage, she waited with a number of other young hopefuls from various countries for her turn to walk out on the stage and sing. She began to ask herself: Am I still in voice? Will I remember the words? How will the judges react to me? Her attack of nerves made her worry about being short of breath or trembly, reactions that would affect the quality of her voice, as would the dry mouth that usually went with nervousness. Then the vivacious brunette who was the assistant to the director of the company called her name, smiled at her, and put a check mark on a piece of yellow paper.

She was in the center of the lighted proscenium stage now, handing her music to the opera's accompanist. She stood tall with her hands folded in front of her, as she had been trained, and heard the free, ringing tones of her voice pour from her throat. The relief of knowing that confidence had come with performance made her relax further, and when she finished she was satisfied with her rendition of the aria.

Half-expecting to be asked for the other song, Marguérite's appeal to heaven from Gounod's *Faust,* she turned to the piano where that score lay. But a voice from out of the shadowy auditorium uttered those implacable, dismissing words, "Thank you, thank you very much," and Diane took her music from the piano and walked off the stage, her heart leaden with the thought that she had failed.

"We have your address?" the assistant asked brightly. Made nervous again by the question, Diane could only nod her response. Perhaps she had a chance after all.

"When will you know?" Greg asked that evening as they sat in the garden after dinner under a black velvet sky.

"Soon," Diane said. "That's one blessing, anyway. I won't have to live in suspense. Denise has connections. She's going to find out how I did and let me know tomorrow."

The thick white candle lit Greg's face. "Is that legal—operatically speaking?"

"No, darling," she trilled, amused by the expression of

concern on his features, "but do you think you could stand living with me for the next month, otherwise?"

He grinned knowingly, then he reached forward and took her hand in his. He kissed the palm and the sensitive underside of her wrist. Tremors of delight ran through her. She seized his hard, rough-skinned hand, curled it into a half-open fist, and filled it with soft, whispery kisses.

"You wouldn't have something in mind, would you, temptress?" he asked.

She gave a tiny sharp bite to his thumb. "We could go dancing, but it's fifteen miles of dangerous curves to the nearest disco."

"I see your point. I'll take my dangerous curves right here."

Laughing, they rose, and with arms around each other passed through the French doors. And not once during the night did Diane think about whether she had passed the audition.

The next morning at nine, Denise Michard phoned. Diane took the call in the morning room, a sun parlor decorated in white and buttercup-yellow where they sometimes ate breakfast. Greg was beside her, and when she replaced the white and gold telephone after a toneless "I understand, thank you, Denise," it was minutes later before she heard his worried "Diane?" She realized then that she had been just sitting, staring blankly ahead of her for a long time, lost in shock and underlying despair. "I didn't make it," she said, but she still didn't turn and face him. She had to be alone in the only way she could manage in order to take in the shattering news.

"I gathered as much. Why? Did she tell you?"

"Some of my technique was faulty. The judges—the director of the company and whomever he called in—thought perhaps my training hadn't been as good as it could have been. But worse, they didn't like the quality of my voice. They thought it wasn't large enough for opera. My bottom notes were thin. And so on and so forth."

As she recited automatically what Denise had said, her

mind was busy trying desperately to salvage something from this explosion, this unexpected blast that had blown all her hopes sky-high. Her *foolish* hopes, she told herself wryly; tough old Madame Daudon had been right about her voice, and all the others wrong. But she could find not a sliver of hope in the wreckage. Even other opera companies were out. She knew plenty of singers who went from audition to audition in Europe, but with a verdict like the one she had just received, if she persevered she would end up like most of them—broke and defeated.

Her spirit quailed before the great yawning emptiness that opened up in front of her. The future was no longer a road. It was a vast, desolate plain leading nowhere. Everything she was, everything that was Diane James, had been poured into opera. What would she do now?

Then she felt Greg's strong arms around her. He cradled her against him and whispered, "I'm sorry, darling." She clung to him, letting herself go in the comforting security of his protection.

"I know you are, Greg." She smiled up at him. "Don't worry. I'll get over it." Her eyes filled with tears in spite of her determination to be stoical. "It's just that I worked so damn hard and wanted it so much." She was close to weeping now, just what she had been intent on avoiding.

"Cry, Diane. Go ahead, you've got a right to."

But she didn't. Instead, she forced back her tears and stiffened in his arms. This was the easy, the dangerous way out. She was a grown-up woman, for pity's sake, not a hurt child to run to a man for succor.

Moreover, with all her rationality, Diane had picked up some of the superstitiousness of an opera singer. It occurred to her that the devastation of her career might be only the first blow of fate. Perhaps her love for Greg was doomed, too.

She searched his face for an answer and met his warmly compassionate eyes looking into hers. "We make beautiful music together, goddess. I'm asking you again. Marry me."

Turning her face away, Diane moved out of his arms

and went to the window. A lump, too big to swallow, blocked her throat. She remembered her intention to go with him to the wedding chapel in Menton after the audition and was glad she hadn't made the promise aloud.

"I can't, Greg. Not now."

"Why not now?" he asked, and she could see he was genuinely puzzled by her refusal. "You don't have a career to think of any longer."

Diane winced. She knew he hadn't made that remark to hurt her; still, it was the flick of a whip over an open wound. "I need time, Greg," she said, her voice broken and hesitant. She flung her arms out awkwardly. "And my own space. I have to stop and figure it all out again—who I am and where I'm going and how I'm going to get there. Opera was my life. Now I have nothing again, as I did when I was married to Mike."

"You have *me*," he said roughly.

Diane shook her head sadly. "But you don't have *me*. Don't you see, I have to put myself together again like Humpty Dumpty."

"I don't see anything but the fact that you're scared witless of making a commitment." An expression of pain crossed his sharp, angry features. "Either that or you don't love me."

"I love you, Greg," she said quietly, "but my love wouldn't be much good to you the way I am now."

"Why don't you let me be the judge of that?" His voice was harsh, but there was so much torment in his midnight-dark eyes that Diane wondered if she could stick to her resolve. She was bone-weary, too, physically exhausted from the rigors of training for the audition and emotionally depleted by her failure. Then she reminded herself that she was fighting for her life, a fight made all the harder by the fact that her adversary was the man she loved. She had abandoned her own individual self for a man once; she wouldn't do it again. And if she had needed a reminder of the perils of male paternalism, his remark about being the judge of her decisions was a red warning light.

"I do my own judging, Greg," she said firmly. "I'm leaving," she continued, her voice quiet and, by an effort of will, steady. "I'm going to Paris. I promised my aunt I'd check on her geraniums," she said with a faint attempt at humor. "And I half-promised Guy and Nadia I'd see their new act."

She had never seen him as he was now. His lithe, supple body had gone rigid with anger. A muscle twitched spasmodically in his lean jaw as he struggled for control. Indicating the phone with his hand in a tight, spare gesture, he said through clenched teeth, "Use the chauffeur." He strode to the door, then turned. His tanned face looked suddenly gaunt; his eyes, black as obsidian, bore into hers. "I'll see you when I see you, Diane," he said, but the jauntiness of the words was nullified by his bitter tone.

She stood there silently and watched him walk out. When his footsteps faded down the hall, she burst into wild, abandoned tears.

## - *13* -

THE LEAVES OF the geraniums were a healthy green, the
blossoms a gutsy red. Madame Bertin stood in the cobble-
stone courtyard of the apartment building and regaled Diane
with gossip about the tenants whose rent she collected for
the owner, whose mail she forwarded when they moved,
and whose comings and goings she watched with shrewd
dark eyes set in a network of wrinkles. Diane listened politely and was purposely vague and forgetful during her own
interrogation. She told the *concierge* that she would be occupying her aunt's apartment for an indefinite period of
time.

She took the Métro to the Left Bank café where Guy and
Nadia were performing. The scene was familiar to her—
a smoky, dimly lit room with tables crowded together and
an audience mostly of students from the nearby Sorbonne.
But there were signs of Guy's new fame, too. The club was
large, and there were many expensively dressed Parisians
among the jeans-clad students.

Diane listened with keen interest to Nadia's sweet but
untrained voice render some simple Breton folk songs as

**143**

Guy accompanied her on the harp. This kind of singing had never appealed to Diane as a career. She had always considered opera the only challenge worthy of all her effort and will and spirit. Yet she would need a job once summer was over. So after she had greeted her friends and Guy had led the way to a table in the back where they could talk, she asked him if he knew of a club that was looking for a singer.

"You didn't pass the audition?" Guy asked, his gray eyes both searching and compassionate.

Diane shook her head. "They thought my voice lacked amplitude, was a little brittle. In short, they didn't want me."

"But perhaps you are a lyric soprano, not a coloratura," Nadia said loyally.

Diane shook her head again. "If there had been a chance, I would have heard about it. The vocal coach I had in Nice knows the judges. She would have told me."

"Other opera houses?" Guy asked tentatively.

"No," Diane said with finality.

Nadia put her hand out impulsively and rested it on Diane's arm. "I'm sorry, Diane. I know how much you wanted this. But you still have Greg—and us."

With a wry smile, Diane answered, "I still have you." Noting Nadia's questioning look, she added quietly, "I'll tell you later."

The girl glanced at her brother then, and Guy nodded. "I know it's not opera, Diane," he said, "but would you care to sing here with me until I can find a replacement for Nadia? Or, if you find that you like it, you can stay until the end of my engagement at the club."

Nadia blushed and bent her head. Her fingers flew to her left hand and a diamond ring as spectacular as the emerald Diane had once worn. "I want to get ready for my wedding, Diane. The banns have already been said. You're still coming, aren't you? It's to be in Saint-Cast."

"Wild horses couldn't keep me away." Diane glanced around the room. "And I'd love to sing here with you, Guy.

I would do it to help you and Nadia out anyway, but it will also give me the chance to see if I like café singing."

"It's a deal, then," Guy said, clasping her hand at the same time that Nadia put her small hand on top of theirs.

The effort of learning new songs and a different style of singing so occupied and fatigued Diane during the next few days that she hardly thought of Greg, and, in spite of her promise, she avoided talking about him with Nadia. Although her friend gave her a questioning glance occasionally, it wasn't difficult to steer clear of the subject, since Nadia wanted to talk about Lyle all the time. Whatever embarrassment the young girl might once have felt about her engagement to Diane's ex-fiancé had disappeared, and Diane often thought, amused, that Lyle was now in the forefront of her life more than he had been when they were engaged.

But the day before she left for Saint-Cast, Nadia visited Diane in her aunt's apartment.

In the midst of their conversation about the wedding, Nadia said abruptly, "I've been waiting very patiently for you to tell me, Diane. What happened between you and Greg?"

"We broke up, that's all."

"Who did this breaking up? Not Greg, I'm sure."

Diane looked candidly into her friend's eyes. "I left him. After I failed the audition, he asked me to marry him and I put him off. I was so broken up, I couldn't give him an answer. I simply couldn't commit myself at that time."

Nadia looked at her sadly. "You are so like your mother, Diane."

"What do you mean? You're too young to have known my mother except perhaps to say hello to when you were a child."

"Of course, but my mother knew her, and when your dad ran off with another woman and your mother would come back to Saint-Cast now and then, looking so pinched and drab, my mother would become very angry. I can remember her saying, 'She was such a beautiful girl and look at her now, shrinking her life into nothingness because of a man.'"

"I haven't done that," Diane answered indignantly. "When my husband died, I studied opera. Now I'll find something else to do."

Nadia shook her sleek little head. "It still comes down to the same thing." She shrugged. "Maybe you thought you were doing the opposite. Instead of a drab little dressmaker, you were going to be a glamorous opera star. But when you keep pushing away the man you love, Diane, what are you doing but shrinking your life?"

Diane stared at her, amazed. "My mother was very brave, she kept going after her husband left her. She raised a daughter all by herself." But as Diane answered her friend, she recalled the dreariness of her mother's life and even her own while she lived at home.

"It would have been braver, I think, Diane, to have chosen love again with another man, not to have played the deserted woman."

A lump formed in Diane's throat as she remembered how often, as a little girl, she had longed for a father. She had even daydreamed that her mother had remarried, and that the three of them were happy and gay together.

"I didn't mean to hurt you," Nadia was saying now. "But Guy and I love you and we are concerned for you."

Bemused by the memories and thoughts that were thronging her mind, Diane said absently, "You haven't hurt me, Nadia. I know you and Guy mean the best for me, as I do for you. Perhaps you're right. I don't know. I'll have to think about it. But everything you've just said is probably futile anyway. Greg is extremely angry with me."

"Give him time," Nadia said softly, looking straight at Diane.

Diane was happy that the "regulars" at the café, many of whom were Bretons living in Paris, accepted her in place of Nadine Kerbellec. And like Nadia, at the end of each show, Diane routinely asked for requests. She had just finished making the announcement one evening when a voice from the dim recesses of the room asked for "The Morning Kiss." Diane's hands turned cold and her heart beat painfully fast. The accent and voice were unmistakable. Greg had found her here in Paris.

Unlike the first time, in her aunt's living room, she sang the poignant song mechanically, not daring to express its lyrical emotion, and when Greg came up to greet her and Guy after the performance, her hand trembled as she put it in his. His expression was so grim, his dark eyes so eagle-fierce, she felt almost afraid of him. Yet knowing him so well, she also saw how sharply his cheekbones pushed against his tanned skin and she noted the mauve shadows under his eyes. She longed to smooth away the deep furrows that ran from the corners of his nose to his lips. She wanted to say she was sorry to have caused him so much pain and explain how necessary her behavior had been at that time. But she didn't dare. True, he had come to her. But whether his anger or his love for her would win out in the struggle that was obviously going on within him was something she couldn't tell.

"I'm sure you two have a lot to talk about," Guy said smoothly, "but first I must discuss with Diane some business in connection with the club. If you will excuse us?" he said politely to Greg.

During the ensuing conversation with Guy, which took place on the stage at one end of the room while Greg stood a little distance away, Diane was conscious of Greg's dark, brooding look. His strong chin jutted out belligerently. The cords in his tanned neck stood out above the open shirt, and he held his powerful shoulders straight and tight.

When they had finished, Guy said good night to Diane with a quizzical look and lifted his hand in a half-salute to Greg. Diane left the stage and slowly walked toward Greg. But she was calm now. Her discussion with Guy had refocused her thoughts, at least temporarily, on her work.

Greg made her come all the way to him, and she resented

that. More sharply than she intended, she said, "How did you find me?"

"I asked your friend Yann."

The sneering way he said "friend" nettled Diane. "Yann's a good friend," she said hotly. "I assume I do have the right to have my own friends," she added sarcastically.

"Yann's a good friend, and that druid you're singing with is a *very* good friend, and Lyle was the best friend of all, wasn't he? Lyle was Mr. Fiancé-Make-No-Waves until he met a real woman, one with the guts for a relationship that was a two-way street; a woman capable of genuine, grown-up love."

Stung by his picture of her as an unloving and immature woman, Diane replied in a voice low and resonant with feeling, "I loved you, Greg."

*"Loved?* Then it's over?"

There was no denying her love for him, but she stood mute, feeling herself at a crossroads and afraid of the consequences of an avowal. In the end, it was her body that spoke for her, telling him by its slight sway, by her gleaming eyes, and by her softly parted lips that she loved him.

"Oh, Diane," he groaned. "I was afraid . . ."

He didn't finish. He leaned forward and pulled her into his arms roughly. Then his mouth was on hers, drawing her into him, his passion draining her of strength so that she had to cling to him to keep herself from falling. He tightened his embrace and lavished her face and hair and neck with wild, possessive kisses.

Finally, he held her away from him and looked full into her face. He shook her lightly and said, "How could you do that, Diane? Leave me—for *any* reason."

"I wasn't behaving very rationally, Greg. The disappointment over not passing the audition sort of threw me out of orbit."

"Rational! You were crazy, woman. Where can we go? When we get there, I'm going to put you under lock and key and not let you out of my sight."

"How about tying me up and getting a German shepherd?"

"Not good enough. I've got a friend in the French Foreign Legion who's dying to come home and do a little guard duty."

She reached up and stroked his face. "Is your friend good-looking?" she asked mischievously.

"Don't tease me," he said darkly, and Diane decided perhaps she'd better not.

They walked out into the soft Paris night and strolled along the boulevards, where the street lights shone like captured moons in the still-thick summer leaves. Sometimes her hand would go to his and slow its restless movements across her back, because they had a long wait ahead of them. They stopped at a sidewalk café, crowded at that late hour with other lovers. Diane ordered a *diablo-menthe*, a splash of bright green mint syrup served with a flask of tap water, and Greg had a *pastis*. When he leaned forward to kiss her, his lips tasted of licorice, and he ordered another one because she said she liked the taste. The couples around them halted their animated conversation from time to time to kiss, too. Kissing was as natural as breathing in Paris.

Looking around her at the other tables, Diane said lightly, "I think love is in the air."

"It damn well isn't any place else. Do you mind telling me why we're tramping the streets of Paris? Don't you have a home? You told me you had. That's why I offered to marry you."

Diane smiled. "We have to wait until midnight."

"You mean, so the coach doesn't turn into a pumpkin?"

She laughed again. "No, until French television goes off the air and Madame Bertin goes to sleep."

His roar of mingled surprise and frustration caused heads to turn. "You mean I've been going out of my mind with my need for you and all the time we've been waiting for some old dame to put her hair up in pink plastic rollers and go to bed?"

"Not 'some old dame'! It's Madame Bertin, the *concierge* of my aunt's apartment building, the most powerful woman in the neighborhood."

"And what will she do, hand you over to the Inquisition if you have a man in the apartment?" Greg rose and, putting his hand under Diane's elbow, lifted her to her feet. "Cinderella, your pumpkin's waiting. So is your Prince Charming. And he doesn't give a damn for Madame Bertin and her two ugly daughters."

"She doesn't have any daughters," Diane mumbled as he hustled her along to the nearest Métro station. "Just a cat and a canary." After a moment's reflection, she said, "Or maybe just a cat. I haven't seen the canary recently."

They were only a few Métro stops away from the apartment, and if it hadn't been Paris, Diane would have been embarrassed by Greg's nuzzling her neck and whispering love words in her ear in the brightly lit subway. Then he was hurrying her through the dark streets and up the stairs of the building. She handed him her key and turned on the lights in the apartment. Then, breathless and laughing, she collapsed on the couch in the living room.

Greg crossed the floor in a few quick strides. With his hands firm on her sides, he lifted her high in the air. One patent-leather pump fell off, and she kicked the other one to the carpet.

He buried his face in the folds of her dress. Then he raised his head and asked, "Where's that sexy nightgown you wore in the villa?"

"Under my pillow." Her eyes narrowed in a tantalizing smile. "I was waiting."

Lowering her until her feet were on the floor, he asked softly, "For whom, Diane? Tell me. I want to hear it."

She wound her arms around his neck and tilted her face to his. "I was waiting for a man who kissed—"

"Like this?" he interrupted, pressing his lips to hers with a sweet urgency.

"Yes," she breathed.

"What else?" he whispered against her hair. "This?"

He tightened his arms around her and pulled her hard against his body. The familiar feel of his large frame and the remembered scent of clean skin and soap, coupled with the slightly sweaty end-of-the-night smell of him, excited her. She regretted the small cloth-covered buttons on her dress that slowed his impatient hands. Then she was stepping out of the dress. His hands were fondling her breasts, the long fingers reaching up under her bra to stroke the smooth flesh and bring their dusky tips to life. With a little moan, Diane swayed against him and opened her mouth like a morning flower to his.

"Was this the kind of man you were waiting for, Diane?" He was kissing her bare shoulders now, leaving moist, warm imprints that made her tingle with pleasure so that she didn't want him to stop.

"Something like that," she teased.

He held her away from him then, his eyes twinkling. "Hey, lady, that's my best technique. I've got testimonials from women all over the world."

"Maybe you should try it again, then," she murmured.

He laughed, but his dark eyes burned with his compelling need. His mouth seized hers roughly. His kisses were ravaging now, and Diane felt a throbbing heat rise within her. She quivered as his hands slid across her shoulders and down the length of her back. They were masterful and possessive, and she wanted to belong to them completely.

He picked her up and, touching his lips to hers, murmured against them in a verbal kiss, "Where's that pillow?"

Her eyes told him, and he carried her through the open door and placed her on the bed. He leaned over her and deftly unhooked and removed her bra. The taffeta half-slip went next. Her pantyhose were last, peeled off slowly with tantalizing movements of his hand.

He feasted his eyes on her then, lying golden in the shaft of warm lamplight from the living room. Slowly, he trailed his lips across her breasts and over her soft belly and lightly down the inside of her thigh. "You're a far country," he murmured huskily, "and I'm your explorer. An ancient sea with no chart but the one I'm making."

Her whole body was tingling now, effervescent and sparkly with excitement. She unbuttoned his shirt and with a sigh of satisfaction curled her fingers in his springy chest hair. She plucked at one nipple with her thumb and forefinger, then put her mouth around it, gently tugging, then tasting it with her tongue. A long shudder racked his big frame, and her hands, hasty on his belt, met his.

"Undress me, Diane," he whispered, taking his hands away.

Seized by a feeling of mischief, she pretended that his zipper was stuck, that the last buttons of his shirt were hard to undo, that she wished he would remove his watch because it scratched her.

"Diane, you witch!" he said. "I'll do it myself." And all his clothes went over the side of the bed until he lay stretched out beside her, clad only in his nylon briefs. The pressure of his hard desire against her excited Diane still further. With one quick sweep of her hands, she rendered him as naked as she was. Then her fingertips played seductively over him, caressing his wide shoulders and tapering torso and strong, hairy thighs.

His responsive groans aroused her to new heights of desire, and as he balanced himself above her, Diane arched herself voluptuously up toward him. But to her surprise, he pinched her playfully and growled, "Not yet, my pretty." Then he chuckled fiendishly. "I'll teach you to play games with Gregory R. Kimball."

She had never heard his middle name. "What's the R for?"

"Revenge," he answered, as he started a rhythmic stroking with his hand that was like a fire licking along her skin. As the lingering touches went up her thigh and Greg's hand found its goal, Diane whimpered with desire and clutched at him.

"Now, Greg?"

"No! The Avenger has spoken."

"Greg!" Diane called out in a warning note that hit high G.

He repeated his devilish laugh and started a deliberate assault on her senses that tantalized her unendurably. His long, supple fingers harvested new delights from the ripest parts of her body. She writhed in sensuous frenzy under these caresses. But as though oblivious to her need, he continued to elicit from her with his questing mouth and venturesome hands a revenge that was as hotly sweet to her as to him.

He was breathing hard now and his body was rigid with self-control. Diane changed her tactics to seductive but small movements under him, and teasing, almost chastely restrained, kisses.

"Sorceress!" he murmured, but he continued to hold back.

"I'm an imprisoned sorceress, Greg. Only you can set me free."

"Say you love me, Diane."

"I love you, Greg." Her mellifluous voice colored the words with all the emotion she felt.

Then, trembling with his own suppressed longing, he held her hips in his hands, lifting her to bury himself deep inside her. His loving thrusts launched them both on a spiraling climb of joy that went through the barriers of previous experience. Diane felt as though the earth were literally falling away below her, that she and Greg, linked together by love, were the world, and nothing existed but the sweet piercing rapture of their union.

It took a long time for them to return to earth, and even longer before Greg said, "Shall we set the date? There's no reason now for us not to marry, is there?"

She ran her hands lovingly across his bare shoulders. "Marriage is a dangerous affair." Drowsy and replete with satisfaction, she had meant her remark to be taken lightly. She was surprised when Greg took his arms from around her and said sternly, "Of course it is. It's supposed to be, damn it." He paused. "It's two different people putting their lives on the line for all of their married life. And I mean *all* their married life, Diane. You're not the only person in the world who believes in monogamy—actual, not just legal, monogamy. Sure we'll fight, but we'll fight because we love each other. If we didn't love each other, we wouldn't fight. One of us would walk out on the other, instead; but I assure you it wouldn't be me—not to leave for good and not to go to another woman. For goodness sake, Diane, can't you get it into that stubborn head of yours that we're two new people? We're not your mother and father, and we're not you and Mike."

His angry lecturing infuriated Diane. "I won't be bullied into marrying you," she said indignantly.

Bitterly, Greg mused, "Maybe I should take what's offered and forget about anything else." He took her in his arms again, and as his hand caressed her breasts, her senses flared under his touch. She started to ache with desire for him. But before she lost all will to resist him, she pushed him away. "That's an insult, Greg," she said in a low, pulsing voice.

"Diane, I'm through trying to prove myself," he said seriously. "I won't ask you again to marry me. The next move is up to you. But I warn you, I won't wait forever."

He moved away from her then, as though putting a seal on his statement. Diane lay wide-eyed, staring up at the ceiling. Could she do it again, she wondered—that dangerous trapeze act that was marriage? Would she and Greg really be able to catch each other in midair? Diane turned to Greg. She put one hand out toward his bare back. She advanced her hand to touch him, to feel his smooth skin, to stroke him, to make love to him and tell him yes, she would marry him.

Then she stopped, her hand poised in space. Suppose she fell? There would be no safety net—no career to deflect her hurt at betrayal, no rigid discipline to absorb the loveless hours. Diane turned away. She still didn't have the nerve for it. Marriage was nothing to rush into. Her decision would have to wait.

# - *14* -

FROM THE DIM recesses of sleep, Diane heard a sound like the closing of a distant door. She reached out a hand, then spread her fingers wide on the vacant sheet. For a moment, she thought it was Mike, stealing in after spending the night in another woman's arms. But the sheet was warm under her hand, and the day was bright against the window curtains. It was Greg who had closed the door—he had left her.

She recalled his anger with her the night before, his warning that his patience was wearing thin. Would he leave her without saying good-bye?

Feeling desolate and uncertain, she jumped out of bed. Then she slipped her hand under the pillow, looking for the nightgown she hadn't put on. As she pulled it out, her hand closed on a crisp piece of paper, dislodged from the bedclothes. Diane picked it up gingerly. The handwriting was Greg's. She started to read the note with a pounding heart. Then she laughed out loud, a glorious whoop of relief. He had only gone out for bread and croissants, and asked her to stay in bed.

"With pleasure, my darling," she said out loud. She found the frothy champagne-colored gown and slipped it on. Then she hopped back into bed, pulled the light summer blanket up to her chin, and gradually relaxed into sleep.

She woke up again to a butterfly kiss across the bridge of her nose, the pungent smell of strong French coffee, and the sight of Greg, beaming down at her and holding a breakfast tray of rolls and coffee.

"I was too late for the *pains au chocolat,* but the croissants are still warm. Did you get my note?"

"Yes, thanks. It took a while to find it." She hesitated, then said ruefully, "I thought you had left me."

If she was seeking assurances, she wasn't getting any, Diane thought. Greg's only answer was a long contemplative look, the visual equivalent of last night's warning that he wouldn't wait forever.

Then he smiled, that broad, happy-go-lucky grin that always warmed and lit his face. "Sit up, goddess, and start eating. These rolls won't stay fresh forever."

"Breakfast in bed!" she said with a laugh, taking the tray from his hands. "I feel spoiled."

"You'd better wait until you taste the coffee before you start congratulating yourself."

He seated himself at the foot of the bed and watched anxiously as she took a sip. "Is it okay?"

Diane managed to swallow the bitter brew without making a face, but she couldn't lie, either. "I think as a coffee maker, you're a better lover," she said mischievously.

A grin flashed white in his brown face again. "I've had better compliments from women who hated me."

"Were there many?"

"Women who hated me? No more than I deserved," he said lightly.

"No. *Women,* silly!"

His brown eyes held her sea-gray ones. "Before I was married, yes; and after my divorce; but during, never."

She felt rebuked somehow and to change the subject went to work on brushing crumbs off her nightgown and the sheets. "It looks as though it snowed croissants here."

"Allow *me*," Greg said gallantly and, leaning forward, eyes gleaming wickedly, with long, lingering strokes of his supple fingers he swept the few remaining croissant crumbs from the lace that covered her creamy breasts and from the sheet under her thigh.

"I think you've got them all," Diane finally said with a giggle, pushing his hand away.

With a deliberation that excited her already teased senses, Greg picked up the breakfast tray and put it on the bedside table. "Not all," he said smoothly. "Here's one I missed." He bent over her and placed his mouth on the appliquéd lace flower that lay on her swelling breast.

She was breathless with delight at the touch of his lips. Nevertheless, she pushed him away with a laughing, "No, Greg! We're going sightseeing today."

"There isn't a sight in Paris to match you in that nightgown," he answered huskily, and bent his head again to ignite a fuse of kisses down her scented throat. Then he took the end of one shoulder tie between his teeth and gave it a little tug. It came undone, and the other followed. The top of the gown fell in a frothy wave around her waist. As Greg looked down at her proudly tilted breasts, he murmured, "beautiful and desirable," and this time Diane rejoiced at her womanly beauty and the happiness it would soon give the man she loved. He kissed the pink buds lightly, tantalizing Diane's nerves with a need for more. Then, with the tip of his tongue, he stroked each one into a lofty little peak. He took one of the taut buds in his mouth then, curling his tongue erotically around it, nibbling gently at it with his teeth. Her breasts began to feel warm and full under his hot kisses. She moved luxuriantly under the hands that were molding the champagne chiffon to her hips and thighs and buttocks. Then he started to peel the gown off her, his hands going first and his lips following to blaze a passionate trail down her midriff to the soft mound below.

She whispered love words to him as the thrill of his caress seared through her. She slid her hands up under his

T-shirt and took it off him so that she might feel his warm skin, smooth as silk over the hard muscles. Then she ran her hands down inside his pants, leaving it to him to undo his belt and zipper. Finally, he was looming above her, his nude body settling over hers. Looking up into the richly hued brown eyes she loved so well, Diane locked her arms around his neck and without hurry pulled him down to her. She closed her eyes during the honey-slow descent of his lips to hers, the better to taste their sweetness when they closed on her languidly parted ones.

He wrapped her close, gently nudging her legs apart with his own. She felt the fullness of his desire and arched her hips upward, tremulous with longing for their union. When it came, in a driving rhythm that was the beat of life itself, she knew that she would tell him—not now but soon— what he so badly wanted to hear.

When they woke up again, it was almost lunchtime.

"Some tour guide!" Greg grumbled facetiously, looking at his watch. "I haven't seen the Louvre or the Eiffel Tower or sent a single postcard."

Diane pushed aside the leg he had thrown over hers in sleep and pulled herself out of the nest he had made for her of his arms. Her eyes shining with fun, she looked down into his face and said, "Suppose I make it up to you with dinner on a *bâteau mouche,* one of those sightseeing boats that go up and down the Seine?"

"Don't you have to sing tonight?" he asked, surprised.

"Oh, I think Guy will let me off for one night."

"You and that Breton baritone are pretty close, aren't you?"

"We're friends, Greg. We grew up together, in a sense."

"Were you ever lovers?" he asked bluntly.

"No. If it's any of your business," she added, nettled by his possessiveness.

"Sure it's my business. I'm the guy who loves you, remember? I'm not jealous of Kerbellec. It's just that you always hold back a little with me, whereas you and Guy seem to share just about everything—childhood, singing, and the whole Breton mystique. You're even ruining your voice for him, singing in that smoky café."

"I *like* singing in that smoky café, and I'm grateful to Guy for giving me a job when I needed one. He could have replaced Nadia with someone else and trained her right from the beginning."

Greg laughed scornfully. "So now you're going to spend your life traipsing around Europe, singing Breton folk songs with the druid."

"If I want to, I will," Diane said defiantly.

But she couldn't quarrel with him. Not today, when the memory of the delight he had given her was so fresh and when Paris lay outside waiting for them. She wound her arms around Greg's neck and said winsomely, "But I don't know if I want to. Besides, lovers shouldn't quarrel—not in Paris."

"Paris! Is that where we are? I thought it was Niagara Falls." He gave her derriere a light, playful slap. "Come on, temptress, put on your tour guide outfit and we'll do the town."

It was a day of high white clouds and blue sky, of sunshine and crisp air with a hint of autumn in it. Agreeing that it was too beautiful a day to spend indoors, they skipped the Louvre and walked in the gardens of the Tuileries just outside it. Although there were yellow leaves on the ground, the trees were still full enough to form a shaded alley and the flowers in the formal gardens burned jewel-bright in the clear air. Diane and Greg ate a *croque-monsieur,* a thick ham and cheese sandwich fried in egg batter, at the umbrella table of an outdoor refreshment stand, then strolled along the sandy path under the trees to the pond where, surrounded by classical statues, generations of Paris children had sailed their toy boats.

They paid a park functionary, an elderly woman with a leather pouch around her waist, for the privilege of occupying two straight-backed metal chairs alongside a row of knitting mothers. Then they watched with rapt interest as a boy in short pants struggled with a large, unwieldy box and finally extracted his boat, an oversized toy submarine.

"My God," Greg said, awestruck. "It's the French nuclear navy." He leaned forward, obviously dying to get his hands on the boat. How happy Greg would be to have a son, Diane thought. How happy *she* would be to bear his child. She daydreamed a little, picturing the two of them with a family. Then Greg was on his feet, showing the boy how to start the motor, but careful, Diane noted, to let the child do it himself. The mother's eyes rested briefly on Diane. Reassured that this foreigner was not alone and therefore not a kidnapper, a terrorist, or a child molester, she beamed at Greg.

When the submarine finally started its maiden voyage across the pond, the little boy and Greg exchanged satisfied smiles. Then, when the boy pressed the radio-control device he held in his hand and the submarine successfully submerged until only its periscope showed, they gravely shook hands.

"Let's go," Greg said, lightly touching Diane on the arm. "I don't want to be here if that sub doesn't surface."

So with smiles and *au revoirs* and polite nods, Greg and Diane wandered off to the broad steps that led out of the park to the vast and beautiful Place de la Concorde. They crossed the Concorde bridge to the Left Bank and strolled along the quays, lined with the green wooden stalls of second-hand-book dealers. They stopped now and then to examine old prints hung with clothespins on a line suspended across the low roof of the stall, or yellowed paperbacks and dusty packages of collectors' stamps. Then they leaned their elbows on the tree-shaded, sun-dappled wall and looked across the Seine to the sunbathers on the opposite quay and the lovers meandering hand in hand, stopping to kiss as the urge seized them.

"When in Rome," Greg said, taking Diane's face in his hands and kissing her tenderly on the lips.

She nuzzled his cheek with her nose. "It's Paris, silly."

"Wherever it is, it's a great way to live. We'll have to come here more often."

We will! Diane thought. And in a few years, we'll bring our little boy to sail his boat in the Tuileries pond. We'll bring *two* boats, she thought impishly—one for his dad. She took Greg's hand and put his arm around her waist as they continued their walk. She felt shy about saying she was ready to marry him. In spite of all reason, some lingering fears remained. But the romantic boat ride tonight would be the best time, anyway.

Exhausted by their afternoon of tramping the streets of Paris, late in the day they sank gratefully onto the wicker chairs of the Café de Flore. The café was famous as a former literary hangout, but Greg and Diane weren't interested in ambiance at the moment.

"What's tall and cool and thirst-quenching?" Greg asked.

"A *citron pressé.*"

"I'll have it, whatever it is."

So at Diane's request, the white-aproned waiter brought two glasses of freshly squeezed lemon juice along with a carafe of water and a few paper packets of sugar. They sat for a long time, sipping the cool drinks, holding hands and kissing from time to time, and watching the ever-fascinating parade of people.

When it was evening, they took the Métro to the Place de l'Alma to board the *bâteau mouche,* a svelte passenger launch with a plexiglass roof and sides. Greg and Diane were shown to their table, nicely appointed with a red cloth, a candle, and crystal wine glasses already in place. As night fell, the boat cast off, to glide slowly past the famous buildings, brightly lit against the dark sky, that lined both banks of the Seine, while a small string ensemble played the song "La Seine" and other popular French melodies.

Greg took Diane's hand in his and raised it to his lips. All the while his eyes searched hers over the shifting dance of the candle flame.

"Happy?" he asked.

"Is ecstatic good enough?"

"It'll do," he said with a grin. He opened her palm then and kissed it, and the feel of his lips on even so mundane a place sent a shiver of delight through her.

"How is the waiter going to serve us if you keep kissing me?" she asked.

Greg shrugged. "That's his problem." He looked around him. "Besides, wouldn't you be embarrassed if we made a spectacle of ourselves by being different?"

Diane glanced around her. Most of the tables were occupied by couples, all of whom were busy with each other in the same way that she and Greg were.

"They're missing the buildings and the beautiful illuminations," Diane said.

"Try telling *them* that!"

Slowly, Diane and Greg worked their way through a three-course dinner bracketed between hors d'oeuvres and an assortment of cheeses. Diane chose *langouste mayonnaise* for her first course, then chateaubriand with *béarnaise* sauce, and finally, for dessert, baked Alaska. But she ate only small quantities of each dish.

"Not hungry?" Greg said.

Diane grimaced. "I can't eat too much because I'm going to have to sing tonight."

"What!" Greg exclaimed. "I thought you got the night off."

Diane shook her head. "I didn't want to spoil our good time by telling you, but Guy asked me to do the last show with him. Some important people will be there, and he wants me to spell him for a while because his voice gets tired toward the end of the night."

"Why can't he just play his harp?"

"Don't be childish, Greg."

"I'm not being childish. I think he's got a lot of nerve pulling you off a date just so his voice won't get tired."

"It wasn't entirely Guy's fault. If you want to know the truth, I offered to come in."

"You offered! You just can't stay away from the place, can you?"

"It isn't that. I know what singing in a smoky room does

to Guy's throat. I thought it was the least I could do for him."

In a low voice, Greg said, "So what it amounts to is that you're more concerned about Guy's throat than about my feelings. I mean, you just walk off a date with me and go running to him because of some silly notion that he needs you."

"I refuse to be owned, Greg," Diane said quietly. "What I do with my life and for my friends is my business."

"Up goes the wall again, the chain-link fence," he said bitterly. "You can be seen through it but not touched; isn't that the idea, goddess?"

"Stop calling me that silly name and stop interfering in my life. I've had enough of it."

Diane was close to tears with disappointment. This was the romantic evening on which she had planned to tell Greg she would marry him. Suddenly everything seemed plastic and tawdry. The waiters walked as if their feet hurt. The string ensemble sounded sugary. The lovers were boring with their constant whispers and pecks at one another. Moreover, the flickering candle flame bothered her eyes.

She leaned forward and blew it out. Then, sitting there in the sudden dark with Greg opposite her, not touching or speaking, Diane was appalled by what she had done. The extinguished candle wick seemed symbolic of what had happened to their love.

When the trip was over and the boat docked again at the Place de l'Alma, Greg insisted on taking Diane to Guy's club. They went by cab and Diane assured Greg that if Guy couldn't see her home, she would be perfectly safe taking a taxi to her aunt's apartment. Standing outside the café, she watched the cab drive off with him, thinking that she would almost rather Greg were jealous of Guy in the usual way than resentful of her closeness to her friend. There would be passion in that kind of jealousy; this seemed only proprietary. She had already experienced with Mike the consequences of trading independence for love. No matter what it cost, she was determined not to do it again.

As she sang that night, her eyes kept moving toward the door in the hope that Greg would return. She even tried to pierce the dark corners, thinking she might have missed him when he walked in.

Guy noticed and, his gray eyes searching hers, asked, "Are you expecting Greg, Diane?"

"Yes. I mean no. We quarreled. I thought he might come back to make up."

"May I ask what you disagreed about?"

Diane laughed awkwardly. "About you, Guy. Greg is jealous." She expected him to laugh with her at the ridiculousness of Greg's attitude. But he just nodded as though this news didn't surprise him. "But it's crazy, Guy. You know there's nothing between us."

"Nothing romantic, Diane, but that doesn't mean nothing at all. A lover can be jealous of a friend or even of a brother."

"Sure, if he's a possessive lover!" Diane shot back."

Guy laughed. "All lovers are possessive, Diane."

Guy's statement triggered a flash of insight in Diane. Lovers *were* possessive—until they were sure of the one they loved. She would probably feel the same way about a similar relationship of Greg's. She glanced at Guy speculatively, remembering the girl he had left in the pines of Saint-Cast when he went to Nadia's rescue. Her childhood friend had become a man of the world.

"Why don't you leave Paris? Go back to Saint-Cast with Greg," Guy said now, his eyes shining with affectionate shrewdness.

"But how will you get along without a female singer?"

"My engagement at this particular club will end soon. Then I'll be going to Saint-Cast myself for Nadia's wedding. After that, I start in a new spot. You can always come back and sing for me, Diane"—Guy hesitated—"if things don't work out between you and Greg."

"They'll work out," Diane said joyfully. "I'm sure of it now." She looked at him fondly. "Thanks, Guy. It's like the old days when we were kids. Big brother straightened me out again." She threw her arms around Guy's neck and hugged him. As she stepped back, she saw Greg where she had been looking for him earlier, standing in the shadows of a dimly lit corner. The interpretation that she knew he would put on her affectionate embrace of Guy and the fact that he had been watching her exploded Diane's just arrived-at understanding into smithereens and infuriated her anew. With fire in her eyes, she said, "Spying on me, Greg?"

"I came to take you home." He glanced toward Guy. "Unless you've made other arrangements."

With a twinkle in his eyes and a sidelong conspiratorial look at Diane, Guy stepped aside. "I promised to meet a friend at the *brasserie* down the street. *Au revoir,* Diane; Greg."

As Greg stood glowering at her, Diane said, "Stop glaring, Greg, it wasn't what you think. I've told you over and over that Guy is a good friend. He just told me he was getting a replacement for me. We can leave Paris tomorrow if you like."

He looked at her for a long time; then he said bitterly, "You've got your men all compartmentalized, haven't you?"

"What do you mean?" she stormed back at him.

"Lyle went well with a career. Guy's your friend and confidant. And I'm your passionate lover." She stared at him aghast, hardly believing he could mean what he had just said. "There's safety in numbers, isn't there, Diane? You can always lop off a friend or a lover and replace him, but loving one man who is all these things is too big an investment for you to make. If you lose him, you lose everything, the way you did with Mike." Then his expression softened a little. "Come on, it's late. I'll take you home."

"I'll take the Métro," she said stiffly.

"Oh, no, you won't, not at this hour."

"I'm leaving." She turned and started to walk out of the empty club.

Suddenly, she was spun around with a fury that made her gasp. His hands gripped her shoulders painfully. "I'm not reading about you in tomorrow's *Trib*, Diane. You're going back to your aunt's apartment with me, and that's final."

Defeated, she couldn't do anything but glare at him. His arrogant interference in her life had gone too far. Where once his touch had caused her whole body to flame up into desire for him, now her high color and flashing eyes, the quick rise and fall of her breasts, and her curled lips expressed only indignant anger.

His stern eyes warmed to undisguised admiration and ardor. He pulled her to him, neither roughly nor gently, but with an authority that quelled any thought of resistance. His lips took hers masterfully, claiming their due. Overwhelmed anew by her love for him and worn out by her seesawing emotions, Diane went passive and limp in his hands. She raised her face for the kisses he rained on it, and for a fleeting moment she thought that this was all she wanted or would ever want from life. But this very passivity, this complete abdication of self, frightened her, and she pulled violently away from him.

A shadow of hurt crossed his face and was gone almost before Diane was sure that's what it had been. "You're not ready to give yourself yet, are you, Diane? I hope when you *are* ready, I'll still be around. I want to marry a whole woman, not just bits and pieces left over from other encounters."

Insulted and angry, Diane struck back through lips scorched by his kiss, "I wouldn't marry you if you were the last man on earth."

# - *15* -

THE DRIVE BACK to Saint-Cast from Paris was an agony for
Diane. The man sitting next to her, his capable brown hands
on the wheel, might have been a stranger for all the warmth
there was between them. They "made" conversation about
the road, the weather, where they should stop for lunch.
Each sat scrupulously in the center of his seat. And there
were no silly jokes or lighthearted bubbly laughter.

They were both right and both wrong, Diane reflected.
Greg was wrong to be jealous of her friendship with Guy,
but right, she reluctantly conceded, about her. She had gotten stuck, like a phonograph needle in a groove, playing
the same theme over and over of distrust and defense against
being hurt again. She had committed the unpardonable sin
of stereotyping people, seeing all men as basically alike just
because the two most important men in her young life had
shared the same defect, a pitiful one when you reflected on
the glorious challenge marital faithfulness was. She had
been right in maintaining her independence, but there was
no point in reminding yourself over and over that you were
your "own woman" if you weren't, as Greg had put it, a

"whole woman." Moreover, Greg hadn't really threatened her independence except when he had been driven to it by his frustration.

She was ready now, she thought, to do that dangerous act on the flying trapeze, to say "I was wrong. I love you and I want to be your wife." But as Greg's coolness toward her continued, she no longer believed that he would catch her if she fell. It seemed as though this time he really was through, and so she said nothing. Besides, she rationalized, she still had no career goal, no new direction, and she really ought to focus on that right now, rather than marriage.

They said good-bye at her aunt's door. Diane insisted she could handle her bags once they were set inside for her. But when the door closed on Greg, she collapsed onto the smart blue ladies' pullman and cried till only dry sobs were left.

The frenetic jangle of the telephone got her up. Her spirits soared with hope. There had been enough time for Greg to reach home. He was calling to bring them together again.

But it was Nadia.

"Diane! Guy told me you were coming back today. Can you come to dinner tomorrow? Lyle will be there, and we both want so much to see you." The sweet, flutelike voice paused a moment. "I've invited Vanessa, too."

"Vanessa is back in Saint-Cast?" Diane asked, surprised.

"Actually, Dinard. She's here for the wedding." Again, there was a hesitation, and Diane had the feeling that Nadia was suppressing a laugh. "She came out of family loyalty, she says. Will you be able to come, then?"

"Yes, of course I'll come. I'd love to," Diane answered. Then, in an effort to break out of her sadness, "How are the wedding preparations going?"

"All right, I guess. *Maman* wants everything the way it's always been in our family. I'm to wear the gown and veil that she and her mother before her wore, and the reception will be at the Grand Hotel in Dinard. It will all be very stuffy and correct. *You* know."

"Yes, I know." But Diane wasn't thinking of the staunch

traditionalism of the Kerbellecs. She felt, rather, the poignancy of regret, the sadness of "what might have been" for her and Greg.

"Remember, tomorrow at seven," Nadia sang out.

"I'll be there."

When she hung up, Diane felt empty inside. She eyed her suitcases but didn't want at the moment to see the clothes she had worn when she was with Greg. She wandered through the rooms, looking for something to do. But she had cleaned well before leaving for Nice and so there were no dull housekeeping jobs to absorb her unhappiness.

Her eye fell on the box of tapes she had made of the impromptu folk concert held in her aunt's living room. A longing came over her for some kind of comfort, some balm for the desolation she felt in the very depths of her being. She took out the tape she had neatly labeled "The Morning Kiss" and pushed it aside. She wasn't ready for that yet. But something was working in her mind, some motivation that was detached from her own misery. Following this tenuous trail, she loaded the cassette player with the songs Guy had sung and the others had played on their instruments. As she listened, her mind went to Greg, as it must since he was never out of her thoughts for long, but this time she focused on his descriptions of the music he had heard in Africa and other places. The Breton songs had been written down and recorded. They would always enrich civilization, but the songs of less-well-known people would be lost to the world as the oral tradition gradually died out. Some of this music had been and was being recorded, but there were never enough people to do this job, particularly as it involved the hardships of travel in undeveloped countries.

Diane's excitement grew as she reflected on her idea. Becoming a musicologist would require going back to school for an advanced degree, but she would welcome that. Afterward, there would be no barrier in her way. She was young and well educated musically, and no softy about living conditions. Diane's eyes gleamed at the prospect of a career that would be both professionally interesting and socially worthwhile. And, she reminded herself sternly, a career in ethnomusicology was more realizable than that of opera star.

Filled with new hope, she went to her suitcases and started to unpack. Each garment brought with it a train of memories. Here was the mini she had on when she and Greg were caught in the sea cave; the white suit she had worn to the Mont-Saint-Michel on the glorious night when they'd consummated their love; the sexy nightgown. She took the length of champagne-colored chiffon and held it in her hands, reliving the rapturous nights she had spent with Greg— nights filled with laughter and sharing as well as physical passion. He had told her about his wife; how, although it seemed at first that they were made for each other, somehow they never really achieved true intimacy. That feeling of recognition, of a rejoining through the loved one of some lost part of oneself, never happened. "Like Lyle and me," Diane had said. And that explained it, Diane mused now, explained her feeling of "death in the soul," as the French described utter desolation. In losing Greg, she had lost a part of herself.

She wrenched her thoughts away from Greg and, to prepare herself for her new career, passed the rest of the day listening to the tapes. But she listened with one ear cocked for the phone, and when it didn't ring, her heart ached dully with disappointment. It didn't ring the next day either. She realized now that he wouldn't call. It was one more thing she would have to accept, she told herself, like her unhappy marriage and Mike's death, and failing the audition. She had a career again, or the prospects of one, but careers were like baskets with only one handle. They were no substitute for love.

That night she dressed with more care than usual and applied more makeup, following the dictum that the worse you felt the more important it was to look good. Giving herself a final inspection in the mirror, she decided that she might not look happy but she did look glamorous. The lavender eyeshadow she had used to go with her purple silk blouse deepened the gray of her eyes, giving them a smoky look. She had lost weight, too, so that the bones of her face stood out in interesting relief. Even her curves seemed more pronounced, juxtaposed as they now were to a smaller waist.

Diane's spirits rose a little at the prospect of the dinner party. She not only looked forward to the enjoyment of being with friends, but was also interested in seeing how Lyle and Nadia behaved together and curious about what Vanessa thought of her brother's sudden change of fiancée. Diane wondered too how shy young Nadia handled that female dragon.

When Diane arrived, she found, as she expected, that the party included Madame Kerbellec, resplendent for the occasion in a blue silk print. With her rotund figure and red cheeks, Nadia's mother always reminded Diane of a Normandy apple. And since Madame Kerbellec spoke only French, Diane foresaw an evening of translation ahead of her.

Diane thought that Lyle's attitude toward her, strangely enough, wasn't much different from what it had been when they were engaged. There was the same chaste kiss, the fond look, and the sense of a benign friend always standing by if needed. Intrigued by this observation, Diane watched him with Nadia and saw at once how different Lyle was as the French woman's fiancé. Now he had the aura of a man confident of his masculine appeal. His behavior toward Nadia even had overtones of seductiveness. And Nadia combined the waiting look of a young girl hovering on the edge of fulfillment with the authority of a soon-to-be-married woman.

Vanessa, to Diane's surprise, was almost effusively friendly. The reason came out when she drew Diane aside and whispered, "I would rather it had been you, Diane. The Kimballs have never had a ... 'foreign influence' in the family."

Diane's mind did a rapid scan of the centuries. Hadn't Lyle mentioned certain immigrant forebears?

"I thought ... a French fur trader?" she said hesitantly. "And wasn't there a Hungarian something or other? Even an Indian chief, as I remember."

"Yes, dear, but they all learned to speak English." Vanessa leaned forward and lowered her voice still further. "This girl hardly understands a word I say."

Diane stared at her perplexed. Nadia's English wasn't *that* bad. In fact, it had even improved since Lyle started helping her, while Nadia, in the spirit of fair exchange, had been teaching him French.

Leaving Madame Kerbellec and Vanessa to stare wordlessly at each other and Lyle to open the bottle of wine on the dining table, Diane went to the kitchen to help Nadia.

"You and Lyle seem supremely happy," she said. "I've never seen Lyle look better. You're obviously very good for him. But . . ." She stared at Nadia, puzzled.

"But . . . you want him back? Is that what you're trying to say, Diane?" Nadia's dark eyes laughed mischievously at her.

Diane laughed, too, a long hearty laugh, the first in days, and it felt good. "He wouldn't come, and you know it. What I wanted to ask is, how do you get along with Vanessa?"

Nadia's delicate features lit with glee. She whispered conspiratorially, "I pretend I don't understand English very well, that I forgot everything I learned when she and Lyle and I traveled around Brittany together." She raised one warning finger. "Don't give me away, Diane."

Diane laughed at the picture of all Vanessa's catty remarks falling on seemingly deaf ears. "Believe me, I won't say a word. But what does Lyle think of your little stratagem?" Was there ever an "ex," Diane mused, who wasn't curious about her former partner's new relationship?

"You know Lyle. He's so sweet and good-natured that anything that keeps people happy and at peace with one another is okay with him." Diane nodded in agreement. Then Nadia gave her a shrewd, assessing look. "He is also one of those men who likes to be bossed a little by a woman."

Curiosity lies on both sides of the fence, Diane told herself. Nadia wants to know if I "lost" her wonderful Lyle because I didn't understand how to treat him. "And that's something I couldn't have done," Diane answered. "Lyle and I simply weren't meant for each other. But judging by how happy you both seem, I think that perhaps you and he were."

"It's funny, isn't it, Diane? Lyle and Greg are brothers, and yet they are very different—so much so that each needs a very different kind of wife."

Diane's clear gray eyes gazed candidly at her friend. "Greg and I are not getting married, Nadia. This time it's final. Our affair is over."

Nadia frowned. "I still think you're making a big mistake, Diane. I'm sure Greg loves you very much."

Diane smiled wryly. "He used to, but when I kept turning him down he cooled off for good. Men have a way of cutting their losses, you know."

"'Men'?" Nadia said. "I thought we were talking about Greg."

So she had been stereotyping again, Diane thought, even after vowing she wouldn't, and little Nadia had been shrewd enough to catch her at it.

Lyle came into the kitchen just then. "Diane, would you mind relieving me in the living room? I've been translating for Madame Kerbellec and Vanessa, and it's like working at the U.N. during an international crisis." Catching sight of his fiancée's troubled expression, he said, "What's wrong?"

"Diane just told me she and Greg aren't going to be married."

Lyle looked at Diane slyly. "Diane, for shame—living in sin. No wonder Vanessa called you a temptress."

Nadia, perplexed, looked at both of them in turn, but Diane smiled back at him. So Lyle had known all along and characteristically had decided not to interfere between her and Vanessa. Diane couldn't imagine Greg's not coming to her defense in a similar situation. Perhaps what she had so often objected to as his "interfering" was just the natural interest taken by a vigorous man in his loved one's life.

"They won't even be doing that," Nadia put in. Then, hand over her mouth, she looked at Diane. "Do you mind? I didn't mean . . ."

Diane laughed. "No harm done. Greg and I are through, Lyle. The affair's over. That's what Nadia meant."

Lyle's light brows came together in a frown. "It won't be awkward for you, will it, Diane?"

"Awkward? What are you talking about?"

"Seeing Greg again. He's coming tonight, of course."

Diane turned to Nadia. "You didn't tell me," she said accusingly.

"But it was understood," Nadia complained. "How could I have a dinner for the family and leave out Greg?"

And how could you invite Greg and not tell me? Diane felt like saying. However, instead of speaking her mind, she seized upon a possible escape. "But I'm not 'family,'" she objected.

"You're as good as," Nadia answered.

"Diane!" Lyle said warningly. "Those two women are sitting there glowering at each other. Go in there and get them trading recipes or something."

Her heart fluttering with anxiety at the thought that she would soon be seeing Greg again, Diane seated herself between Madame Kerbellec and Vanessa like a referee and directed the conversation to what she thought was the innocuous subject of flowers. Even this, however, turned out to be an occasion for rivalry, since each woman claimed a garden roughly the size of Wrigley Field.

Diane kept a polite smile on her face and disbelief out of her eyes as she turned from one to the other like a tennis spectator, translating only the more complimentary phrases and leaving unsaid charges of "Texas-type exaggeration," Madame Kerbellec having a weak notion of the geography of America, and from the other side "the disregard for the truth so often exhibited by foreigners."

Diane didn't think she could stand to see Greg, to have him courteous and distant with her as he had been on the drive from Paris. She thought of making some excuse—

any excuse—and leaving, but then as the minutes passed and he still hadn't arrived, she decided that perhaps he had forgotten the date. Or maybe he didn't want to see her, either.

She had relaxed so much in the expectation that he wouldn't come that when the doorbell rang, she jumped, and Vanessa fixed her with a questioning look. Then she heard Greg's deep baritone, his apology for being late, and Nadia's sweet-voiced thanks for his flowers. Usually warm-blooded, Diane felt her hands and feet go cold with nervousness. She felt pale and unsettled. She stopped translating some bit of nonsense in midsentence and tried to compose herself for Greg's entrance.

Her training for the stage gave her the discipline she needed. Graciously, she put her hand out to Greg and smiled.

"Welcome to the family get-together," she said lightly.

"I guess we've finally been taken off that desert island." His tone was as easy as her own, but his dark eyes looked sunken, as though he hadn't been sleeping well.

"Whatever are you two talking about?" Vanessa said, annoyed. "Really, when even English-speaking people don't make sense!"

"It's a private language, Vanessa, like the ones twins and ex-lovers use," Greg said cryptically.

Diane flinched under his attack, even though Greg dropped his voice so that she was the only one who could hear him. She had no retort ready. She only wished numbly for a quick end to the dinner and the torment of sitting beside him, so close that their hands couldn't help but touch from time to time as they passed the platter of roast lamb and the other dishes Nadia had spent days getting ready.

Everything was praised, and rightly so since the food had been both imaginatively and well prepared. It not only tasted good but was artistically arranged and garnished. Morever, Nadia's decoratively set table was a delight to the eye.

Diane was proud of her friend, and she wasn't alone. Madame Kerbellec seemed to expand like a pouter pigeon in her print silk. She kept darting glances at her rival to see her response. Vanessa, with good midwestern common sense, was digging into the delicious food and obviously enjoying it.

But the absent member of the Kerbellec family was not to be overlooked either, and Nadia's mother soon began boasting about Guy.

"Oh, no! Not my son the folk singer," Greg murmured to Diane.

Her laugh was arrested by Vanessa's high nasal voice returning Madame Kerbellec's volley by extolling Diane's accomplishments as a singer.

Diane was speechless with amazement to hear Vanessa praise her, even for competitive reasons.

"It was a great opportunity for you, Diane, was it not, to sing with Guy this summer?" Madame Kerbellec was obviously bent on keeping the score even.

"It was very agreeable," Diane answered noncommittally.

"Only agreeable?" Greg said. "I thought living in Paris and singing in a café were your idea of heaven."

Anger began to mount in Diane, but she forced herself to cool down. Some idea about her was at work in Greg. She didn't know what it was, but she intended to find out.

The rest of the dinner passed without incident except for the time that Greg's long muscular thigh brushed hers and they both shivered as though they had been branded with the same mark. Claiming a business call he was expecting, Greg left as soon as dinner was over. Diane's offer to help with the dishes was treated as an insult by Madame Kerbellec. Hadn't Diane noticed the automatic dishwasher while she was in the kitchen? It wasn't only Americans who had the latest appliances.

Tired of Vanessa and Madame Kerbellec's disputatious company, Diane joined Lyle where he stood by the window, gazing out at the street.

"Will you go back to Paris, Diane?" he asked. "I didn't know you were so crazy about café singing."

"I'm not, but it seems to be Greg's impression that I am," Diane said wryly. "To be honest, though, I suppose he got it from me. My pride was hurt when I failed the audition. I didn't want him to think my singing in a cellar club was a comedown, so I pretended to like it more than I did. But the part about Paris was true. I love the old city." She shrugged. "I suppose basically I'm an urban person. I can go only so long without theaters and music and street life."

"That's what Greg said."

"What!" Diane replied sharply. "What did Greg say?"

"That he had lost one wife because she couldn't stand the physical isolation of the places he had to go to, that he had recovered fairly readily but that he didn't think he could stand losing you."

Diane's spirits took wing. He loved her, after all. This was the clue she had been looking for, the misunderstanding that was keeping them apart.

She looked at Lyle with an ironic smile. "I'm going to become an ethnic musicologist. I probably won't see a civilized place for years."

"Does Greg know?"

Diane shook her head. "I decided only yesterday."

"Tell him, for heaven's sake!"

"I can't, Lyle. I can't go to him first. I don't have that kind of nerve. If he rejected me . . ." She didn't finish, but she thought, I can't get on that trapeze if I don't know he's waiting to catch me.

"I suppose I could tell him," Lyle said reluctantly.

Diane suppressed a smile. Lyle was his own kind of Jekyll and Hyde, an aggressive, enterprising man of business and a spectator when it came to personal affairs.

"Tell him what?" Nadia had come up to them, unobserved.

Diane answered in a litany of joy, "That I love Greg and I want to marry him and I'm willing to spend years in the jungle, or wherever, with him, because I plan to collect the music of so-called primitive societies."

"Of course Lyle will tell Greg that, if you want him to. Won't you, Lyle?"

This time Diane grinned broadly as her ex-fiancé firmly announced that he would do whatever his present fiancée wanted, and right away.

But the phone still didn't ring—not that day or the next. And finally, unable to bear the torment of waiting, Diane called Lyle.

"He said something cryptic about there being no guarantees in life. He also said that marriage was a dangerous state, but I didn't particularly want to listen to that. Any further message, now that Nadia has made me a go-between?"

"No, but thanks, Lyle. Thanks a lot."

She hung up and started pacing the rooms. This time she was really through. She knew what he was getting at—grow up; learn to trust; you've got to give to get. But she had gone to him first, through Lyle, and he had rejected her. She wouldn't give him a second chance to turn her down.

Then she wheeled sharply around. Hadn't *he* come to *her* again and again, asking her to marry him, and hadn't *she* always said no? If he could take chances, why couldn't she?

Diane marched to the ugly black telephone and dialed the Poilvets' number. It was busy, and she hung up. A second later, the phone's strident jangle filled the house.

She raised the receiver dispiritedly. She didn't want to talk to Lyle or Nadia, or anyone.

It was Greg. "I hate to bother you, goddess, when you're busy transcribing music for the Breton fertility rites, but you know those pictures in the living room, the ones of a three-master in a storm and a lighthouse at sunset that the Poilvets so artistically hung six inches from the ceiling?"

Diane repressed a giggle and said yes.

"Well, they fell down."

"Did they break?" Diane asked, seriously concerned now.

"Unfortunately, no."

"How did they fall?"

"I have no idea." Greg's usual warm tone had gone bland. "But I think you should come over and help me put them up again. I'd hate to see works of art like those badly hung."

Diane couldn't trust herself to answer for a moment. She thought she had lost his love, but she hadn't. It was like being pulled back from the edge of a chasm.

"I'm not sure I should be in your house alone with you, sir," she said in a Victorian simper.

"Suppose I made an honest woman of you?" Under the joking tone, she could hear a note of pleading, of fear that perhaps even now she would say no again.

"Just making a whole woman of me was enough," she said softly.

"Then it's settled," he said, and she could hear the catch in his deep voice. "We'll get married just as soon as we can. Right, Diane?"

"So right, darling," she crooned from the depths of her happiness.

"And honeymoon in the villa?"

Her answer was a delighted "Yes!"

"Listen, I'm coming right over. This phone that I'm holding in a death grip isn't what you'd call caressable."

"How about the Poilvets' pictures?"

"They look better on the floor."

Diane laughed. "I'm coming to you, Greg. It's my job, my duty." She lowered her voice to a whisper. "My love, my delight."

She hung up and backed the old Deux Chevaux out of the one-car garage behind her aunt's house. As she drove, she noticed the brown and gold leaves on the lawns, the schoolchildren going home with their satchels on their backs, the metal shutters on the summer homes.

Poised on the edge of so much happiness, she was afraid. What if he weren't there? What if he had changed his mind? No fear was too unreasonable to be seized upon, examined briefly, then tentatively tossed aside.

But when she saw him waiting at the door for her, his

dark curly hair mussed as though he had run his hands
through it dozens of times since she called and his eyes
shining with love, she experienced a sense of inevitability.
She had been foolish to worry. They couldn't have stayed
apart. Truly, they had been made for each other.

He scooped her up in his strong arms and started to carry
her across the threshold.

"The neighbors!" she said.

He stopped and looked around at the straight pine trees.
"What neighbors? There aren't any." He looked down into
her face, sternly. "Are you always going to give me a hard
time?"

She reached and linked her hands behind his head, and
her knit top rippled over her breasts. "Probably," she said
with a light laugh.

"Undoubtedly," he replied dryly, his eyes scanning her
longingly. "Shall I carry you across the Poilvets' threshold
or not?"

"We're not married yet."

"Almost. As soon as we hung up, I called the mayor's
office to see what's required. With your record, I'm not
taking any chances on your changing your mind."

Still in his arms, she shifted position a little. "I'll never
change my mind, Greg," she vowed. He bent his head then
and kissed her tenderly. Her breasts, which had ached so
for his caress, felt the assuaging stroke of his hand. She
half closed her eyes against the glowing ardor in his, relishing the anticipation, the sure knowledge that they would
soon be joined in the ultimate act of love.

But Greg wasn't heading for the bedroom.

"Where did we first meet?" he asked.

"On the beach."

His lips were against her hair now, his voice husky and
low. "Where did we first touch, first know, first catch fire?"

Diane had relived that moment many times—the shock
that had passed through them both that day, so long ago it
seemed, that they had brushed against each other by the *lit
clos*.

He held her now in one strong arm and slid open the polished wood panel of the cupboard-bed with the other. "We'll be safe against farm animals here, and believe me it's private."

Then he put her gently down on the fresh-smelling feather bed. He undressed her with exquisite slowness until her breasts, tip-tilted like flower petals, shone white in the dark and she lay waiting for him.

"You can put my clothes in the bench," Diane said with a giggle. "Another advantage of the *lit clos.*"

"I think you work for the company that makes them," he growled. "Undress me, wench—but fast! I've waited a long time for you."

"Practice makes perfect," she simpered, as she unbuckled his belt.

"I'll have you perfect in no time," he murmured seductively.

But then she had trouble with the zipper and lost patience and said, "Do you wear a loincloth when you build those hydroelectric dams in the tropics?"

"Always," he said gravely, removing her hands and doing the job himself. "And you'll have to, too, or the headhunters won't recognize you as my wife and they'll eat you."

He bent his head to her and pretended to take huge bites. The touch of his lips on her skin and the gentle savagery of his love bites thrilled Diane, and she moved voluptuously under him.

"Diane," he murmured. "My own beautiful Diane."

He was now as naked as she, and Diane ran her hands down his muscled back and smooth flanks with a contentment that went to the core of her being.

He gasped under her touch and, leaning over her, lifted her breasts in his hands as though they were trophies he had just won. Then he kissed each sleepy nipple, bringing them to life with gentle strokes of his velvety tongue.

"I love you, Diane," he said. "Now and forever. You and only you. My temptress, my sorceress, goddess, my Diane. I also love you here," he added, kissing her breasts reverently. "And here. And here." His lips against her rounded hips and sleek thighs and on the vortex of feminine mysteries between them fired her senses into a frenzy of longing. Her desire was made even sweeter by her new sense of sureness. He had seen the best and the worst of her. He had never ceased to love her. And she knew this about him: He would never hurt her; she would always be able to trust him.

"And I love you, Greg, as I always have, even when I didn't know it." She smiled there in the dark and said mischievously as she touched him all over with her soft hand, "I loved you even when you interfered . . . I loved you even when you were right . . . and I even loved your male arrogance."

He stopped her wandering hand with his. "Temptress!" he said, laughing in his free-spirited pagan way. He settled himself over her then, and as their bodies joined in ecstatic union, Diane heard the drumming of the first rains of autumn against the window.

Later, cradled in each other's arms, they talked.

"Why did it take you so long to call after Lyle gave you my message?" she asked.

"I wanted you to be sure this time."

"I called you first, but your line was busy."

"I was calling you."

"It will all work out beautifully, won't it, Greg? I'll go to school while you build your minihydros. Then we'll start traveling together." She sat up and, leaning over him, drew one finger slowly along his lower lip. "You *will* arrange to build your dams where there's interesting folk music to be recorded, won't you, dearest?"

Grabbing her finger, he answered, "Of course. That's where dams are always built." He sat up abruptly. "Hey, come to think of it, you still haven't seen the Rance tidal-power plant."

Diane put her hands on his bare shoulders and gently

pressed him back against the pillow. Then she slid down beside him and wound her arms seductively around his waist. "How about tomorrow, darling?"

"Temptress!" he breathed as his lips seized hers.

____ 07215-X **JADE TIDE #127** Jena Hunt $1.95
____ 07216-8 **THE MARRYING KIND #128** Jocelyn Day $1.95
____ 07217-6 **CONQUERING EMBRACE #129** Ariel Tierney $1.95
____ 07218-4 **ELUSIVE DAWN #130** Kay Robbins $1.95
____ 07219-2 **ON WINGS OF PASSION #131** Beth Brookes $1.95
____ 07220-6 **WITH NO REGRETS #132** Nuria Wood $1.95
____ 07221-4 **CHERISHED MOMENTS #133** Sarah Ashley $1.95
____ 07222-2 **PARISIAN NIGHTS #134** Susanna Collins $1.95
____ 07233-0 **GOLDEN ILLUSIONS #135** Sarah Crewe $1.95
____ 07224-9 **ENTWINED DESTINIES #136** Rachel Wayne $1.95
____ 07225-7 **TEMPTATION'S KISS #137** Sandra Brown $1.95
____ 07226-5 **SOUTHERN PLEASURES #138** Daisy Logan $1.95
____ 07227-3 **FORBIDDEN MELODY #139** Nicola Andrews $1.95
____ 07228-1 **INNOCENT SEDUCTION #140** Cally Hughes $1.95
____ 07229-X **SEASON OF DESIRE #141** Jan Mathews $1.95
____ 07230-3 **HEARTS DIVIDED #142** Francine Rivers $1.95
____ 07231-1 **A SPLENDID OBSESSION #143** Francesca Sinclaire $1.95
____ 07232-X **REACH FOR TOMORROW #144** Mary Haskell $1.95
____ 07233-8 **CLAIMED BY RAPTURE #145** Marie Charles $1.95
____ 07234-6 **A TASTE FOR LOVING #146** Frances Davies $1.95
____ 07235-4 **PROUD POSSESSION #147** Jena Hunt $1.95
____ 07236-2 **SILKEN TREMORS #148** Sybil LeGrand $1.95
____ 07237-0 **A DARING PROPOSITION #149** Jeanne Grant $1.95
____ 07238-9 **ISLAND FIRES #150** Jocelyn Day $1.95
____ 07239-7 **MOONLIGHT ON THE BAY #151** Maggie Peck $1.95
____ 07240-0 **ONCE MORE WITH FEELING #152** Melinda Harris $1.95
____ 07241-9 **INTIMATE SCOUNDRELS #153** Cathy Thacker $1.95
____ 07242-7 **STRANGER IN PARADISE #154** Laurel Blake $1.95
____ 07243-5 **KISSED BY MAGIC #155** Kay Robbins $1.95
____ 07244-3 **LOVESTRUCK #156** Margot Leslie $1.95
____ 07245-1 **DEEP IN THE HEART #157** Lynn Lawrence $1.95
____ 07246-X **SEASON OF MARRIAGE #158** Diane Crawford $1.95
____ 07247-8 **THE LOVING TOUCH #159** Aimée Duvall $1.95
____ 07575-2 **TENDER TRAP #160** Charlotte Hines $1.95
____ 07576-0 **EARTHLY SPLENDOR #161** Sharon Francis $1.95
____ 07577-9 **MIDSUMMER MAGIC #162** Kate Nevins $1.95
____ 07578-7 **SWEET BLISS #163** Daisy Logan $1.95
____ 07579-5 **TEMPEST IN EDEN #164** Sandra Brown $1.95
____ 07580-9 **STARRY EYED #165** Maureen Norris #1.95

# WHAT READERS SAY ABOUT
# SECOND CHANCE AT LOVE BOOKS